NEHANDA

a novel

Yvonne Vera

We acknowledge the support of the Canada Council for the Arts
for our publishing program.
We also acknowledge support from the Ontario Arts Council.

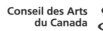

Conseil des Arts
du Canada

Canada Council
for the Arts

ONTARIO ARTS COUNCIL
CONSEIL DES ARTS DE L'ONTARIO

First published in 1993 by Baobab Books, Harare, Zimbabwe.

Library and Archives Canada Cataloguing in Publication

Vera, Yvonne
    Nehanda / Yvonne Vera.

ISBN 978-0-920661-41-3

    I. Title.

PS9390.9.V47N4   1994   823   C94-932242-3

Printed in Canada by Coach House Printing

TSAR Publications
P. O. Box 6996, Station A
Toronto, Ontario M5W 1X7
Canada

www.tsarbooks.com

This book is dedicated to *Kupukile Mlambo*, for many years of kinship and inspiration, my gratitude is too heavy for the mouth to carry with wisdom.

Yvonne Vera
April 1993

1

Ants pull carcasses into a hole, and she is not surprised. Pain sears the lines on her palms, and she turns her eyes to her hands in wonder. Rivers and trees cover her palms; the trees are lifeless and the rivers dry. Anthills move in dying elongated shadows while furious red clouds escape, swirl upward, thin into a haze. Grass trembles with the wind while ants vanish into the ground, over her waiting palms.

Nehanda carries her bag of words in a pouch that lies tied around her waist. She wears some along her arms. Words and bones. Words fall into dreaming, into night. She hears the bones fall in the silence. She is surrounded by a turmoil of echoes which ascends night and sky. In the morning, a horizon of rock, of dry bones, grows into day.

Nehanda waits in the silence. Her throat is parched, like the barren land. The wind has eaten the soil, flung it into the horizon. The grass has been forgotten by the rain. Water gathers in

her eyes, which have been filled with dark heavy clouds, and it is as though it has rained. A storm breaks, and the ground beneath her trembles mercilessly. The wind carries clouds of broken leaves to the waiting horizon.

She feels that gaping wound everywhere. The wound has been shifting all over her body and she can no longer find it. She raises her hands above her head as though supporting a falling roof. She gestures into the sky with frantic arms. She laughs. The skin tears away from her, and she knows that the damage to herself is now irreversible. Nothing will save her from this final crimson of death; it is too much like her inner self.

2

The first time she walked, a gust of wind nearly carried her off. Mother saw and heard the towering cone of swirling dust speeding toward them like an hallucination. It was nodding like a spirit, and its widening skirts turned madly in the frenzy of its own dance. It swirled in spiralling circles conscious of destruction. Through its passionate energy, the thing looked frightening and unnatural. Always, it held the sign that it had been newly created, that it was among the newborn: it raged therefore with an innocence.

Arrogant in its own conception, it challenged the familiar categories of birth and death. It moved at once in opposite directions, with time and against time, collapsing all time within its perturbed interior. Would the transient creature live long enough to reach them? Would it outlive its own death?

The whirlwind measured time in swift motions, effacing distances as it dug the ground with its insatiable belly. Mother panicked at the ferocity of the approaching phantom air. With a dust-filled scream she retrieved her young one whom she cradled in her protective arms and took into the safety of the hut.

She had emerged from the turbulent air transformed into a pillar of dust.

The child watched the wind come toward them. A voice rose from beneath the earth. She saw birth and death, and the presence of her ancestors. The wind was full of the sun. She heard it call to her with its song which emanated from within her: the spirits had presided over her birth.

3

The calabash, which holds the memories of the future, carries signs of lasting beauty. Forgetting is not easy for those who travel in both directions of time.

The harsh smell of fresh cow-dung filled the air; it had been smeared generously on the floor of the hut.

The departed had come to deliver a gift to the living, to shape the birth of voices, to grant the safe passage of the unborn.

Three women wove a circle of strength around the central hearth where a fire sent blue and yellow flames to the dim edges of the small hut. A calabash filled with herbs, covered with wide *mopani* leaves, awaited the birth from beside the square grass mat where the panting mother lay. The vessel's smooth surface had been rubbed with a paste of grey ash; it was woven with red and black beads. The curved handle of a long wooden spoon protruded from the mouth of the pot, amidst the leaves, and often one of the women would rise and stir the contents. The stirring was done with great caution.

The circle of women asserted their strength through their calm postures, waiting. They looked upon their presence in this enclosure as a gift; this was not a chance for them to fail or to succeed; it was a time to rejoice, or else to mourn. They knew that the birth of the child, for whom they all waited, was something that they did not have the power to control. They were here to accompany the mother, and the child, on their separate journeys. No one is allowed to make a journey alone.

The first woman was firm-limbed with long arms covered in thick bangles of engraved wood and ivory. Long, horn-shaped ivory earrings hung above her bare shoulders. If the light had been sharper, it would have been possible to see several circling marks on her wide forehead, which distinguished her from the rest of the women. She belonged to the village only through marriage, an event that had taken place three years previously.

Next to her a woman sat with legs stretched firmly before her, and arms folded protectively across her small breasts. She sang as she carried water in a large rounded vessel on her head from the river to her hut. The day's waiting was perhaps more difficult for her than for the others because for her it was unnatural to sit still.

A third woman knelt by the fire, stirring some porridge in a black clay pot. A trader, she knew where the best markets were, and how people lived in far-flung villages. She laughed easily, showing wide gaps of missing teeth behind her lower lip. Because she was a widow she had a circle of huts, and land to plant her crops. When she was not stirring the porridge she sat on a low wooden stool that had been brought earlier into the hut. Her knees were parted and her cloth fell to the ground between her feet. She had no qualms about sitting on a stool like a man.

The entrance to the hut was blocked by a wide wooden door that was supported from the inside by a big flat rock on which the midwife, Vatete, sat. She was the most important of the human presences in the room. She was as silent as the shadow which climbed the wall behind her back.

4

A harmony of curling black and silver hair covered her head. Her piercing eyes moved rapidly across the room, though the thin skin around them was loosened by age. Her brow was deeply furrowed; and wrinkled pouches, containing many memories, hung below her eyes. Her brow too, carried deep secretive furrows. She had tucked some of her secrets into the folds of skin around her knees and ankles, and around her elbows. Her arms were surprisingly strong.

Vatete was highly respected. When she failed to deliver a child safely into the world, it was understood that the spirits had intervened in the occurrence. For no matter how powerful and ambitious a mortal might be, the departed were in control. They determined who came into the world, and who did not.

The women were here to welcome the child. Each of them had already met the child in dreams which they could not recall. By visiting their dreams, the child had picked them out to receive her. If she had not wanted them, she would have kept them away from her birth. By their ungrudging presence the women had tied themselves irrevocably to the future of the child whom they had not yet seen. In the future, others would recognize the child by her gifts and her difference—her eyes that would see distances. Her eyes would brim with dancing prophecies of hope and despair.

In this smoke-filled hut with its reluctant yellow light, a young woman was lying along the edge of the mud wall, close to the raised mud platform on which the cooking utensils were kept. A series of rounded pots were piled delicately one on top of the other to a height that nearly reached the thatching, successively curving inward and outward to create a tall figure which filled her imagination with wonders of her existence.

She slept on a wide grass mat with a low flat stool supporting her head. She was completely naked. The night was warm and her heels rested on a small black-haired goatskin which would later be used to make an apron to carry the child. The light that fell on her tired face revealed that her wrinkled brow was beaded with sweat. Though this was her first child, she was fortified by the presence of the other women.

"Did you say you walked for two days to arrive at the trading place?" the listeners asked, trustfully patting the dung-covered ground with open palms. With one mouth, the first two women questioned the trader, and moved closer together, their shoulders touching.

"I said it took two days. That does not mean we walked for two days."

"Do not hide your words, like ripe fruit in a tree. Tell us your true meaning."

"That is the time it took before we could arrive, but I do not know how long we walked. We walked part of the time, and part of the time we rested. How much time is that?" She mocked her companions whom she knew had travelled little beyond their own homesteads.

"You forgot to say that some of the time you were lost! Time is not something you can retrieve from behind an anthill after you have been lost all day. But then, only the owner of the dream knows what wonders have happened in dream."

"Have you known a traveller who did not lose the way at least once? Unless you have walked the path before, how can you not get lost some of the time? Even an ant-eater, which is the rarest of wild animals, is one day seen crossing the clearing which surrounds a homestead, before the sun has gone to its mother. Is the ant-eater in search of human company or is it lost?" She answered defensively.

"Perhaps we should say it took you only half a day to arrive. In dream, the spaces between event and event are full of darkness. Only the departed can tell us how to journey through them. One does not ask what causes the skin of the chameleon to change. There are some mysteries which it is good to hide from the eye."

"How long did it take you to return? Was the journey forward the same as the journey back? Did you lose your way on returning as you did going?" the first woman asked. She clapped her hands emphatically, her ivory earring visible in the dark.

"Only the crab knows its own journey, if it is going forward or backward."

"Did you dream this dream for many nights or on one night alone' '. . . Let us stand in the shade a while . . .' '. . . Let us eat the food we packed . . .' '. . . There! A snake along the road . . . let us kill it or else we shall have bad fortune . . .' '. . . Do not talk near this hill or else you will bring us ill fortune . . .' '. . . If you talk while crossing this river you shall lose your gift of speech . . .' There are diversions, surprises, promises, killings, and intervals of conversation that one wonders how the story is ever told to its end, or the journey completed."

The fire rose, the porridge bubbled angrily and spilled into the flames. "Well then, we did go, and we did return. Do you want to know what we saw?"

Soft painful sounds made the women pause in their speech. The midwife had kept her attention fully focused on the mat where the mother rested. After much fumbling and feeling around her skirts for a tiny bottle tied in a cloth, she released some brown powdered snuff which fell weightlessly to the ground. She called upon the protectors of the unborn. "Do not abandon us," she pleaded. "We are your children." With cupped hands, she accompanied her plea with rapid clapping. The women chanted praise names of the mother's lineage, in unison.

For a whole day the women refused to see the sun. The room had changed from silvery grey to complete darkness. After the moon came out, showers of gay light dotted the room. They shone brilliantly whenever the fire died down. The women had willingly escaped the circle of time and claimed a temporal cohesion that did not permit intrusion. They had banished the sight of moving shadows and habitual activity, and sustained their wait with conversation intercepted by singing. The mother looked away from the flame and into the thatching, but could not see the ancestral spirits whose presence fulfilled a duty to the future of their clan.

The midwife saw only her snuff, and the mother. Sometimes she closed her eyes and transported herself to the *dare*, the village fireplace, where she was often invited by the elders to arbitrate in matters of the village, especially those concerning women. The *dare* was a large clearing in the centre of the village. Those who were admitted to the *dare* knew the power of words. The midwife was also among the shapers of wisdom, who determined the future of the village. The mud-plastered wall of the hut was black with continual fires. When smoke went into the midwife's eyes, she rubbed vigorously with her snuff-covered hands, but without effect. The darkness of the hut was in her eyes. The chanting had returned the spirits to their midst.

"Tell us then. Tell us of these wonders you saw at the end of your journey." The two women spoke after a long silence.

"I did not say there were wonders, but we were surprised." She moved the stool on which she sat closer to the fire. The cock broke the silence with prolonged crowing that circled the night. Another responded aggressively in a higher pitch, and that set off a series of cacophonous cries that brought the night closer to the day.

"A surprise and not a wonder? You mean to lose us with your mouth?" the listeners asked.

"Only to tell a tale. We were indeed surprised by what we saw. We thought our eyes had abandoned us. Make me remember, was it not said by the late chief that our kindness would be our death?"

"You met the symbol of death on your journey's path? Is that what you saw? Did something cross your path then?" The two women swallowed more distance between themselves and the story-teller. They now sat very close together.

"If it had crossed our path and passed, we would have been satisfied, and cleansed ourselves in the river. That is not what chanced. We saw the sign, but the sign had decided to live among us."

"Was it a sign? What did you see? Here we stand in the middle of the river. Tell us what you witnessed." The women reached toward the story-teller and shook her shoulders with impatience, as though to wake her. There was panic in their voices.

"The sign was in the form of a human being. A stranger, but a human nevertheless."

"Your sign was a human being? Indeed, this is a tale that calls for another telling. When did human beings . . . with two legs . . . turn into signs? Tell us again, did you say that your sign was a human?" They waved their hands bewildered, suggesting perhaps that signs were expected only to descend from the heavens like birds.

"A stranger, but a human being that we could recognize," she repeated.

"Did the stranger walk on two legs? For how else does a stranger become a sign? Did he walk on two legs or on four? Did he walk forward or backward?"

"The stranger had decided to stay. Did you not hear me tell you of it? We discovered that the stranger had decided to stay among us. The stranger became a sign of our future. What does it mean to have a stranger, with unknown customs, live among you? To live I say, not to visit?"

"That is indeed a sign."

The story-teller sat with her head resting between her palms. "The stranger decided to stay among us. There was evidence all over the hill that the stranger was to be among us for a long time. He had built a home. Humans are not like birds, which build nests in trees only to abandon them in the next season. Humans make homes so that their young may walk the same soil that they have walked. He had taken many cattle away from us. He had moved us into the barren part of our land where crops would not grow. Many people were killed by the stranger. When we saw his arrival we gave him pieces of gold, and he gave us that which he had brought from his own land. What we saw on that hill tied our mouths, and we left in silence."

The fire died down. Darkness grew. A brief silence freed them.

"You say this place was on the hill? Why would the stranger choose to build on the hill, instead of below it? A visitor to a strange land must be humble enough not to choose the highest ground in the land to build his home. These people could not have known our custom."

The dream brought with it no solution. Perhaps they should present the dream to the *dare*, but they feared that according the dream more seriousness would make it more potent. "The elders say that what you have dreamt you have dreamt, do not awaken it. Perhaps the dream means we will prosper in the future. Our kindness shall be our death."

A murmur was heard from the entrance of the hut. The spirits were there. They hovered over the birth unseen and placed gifts of the future on the head of the newborn. The child came silently into the darkness and warmth of the hut. After she had been born she did not cry for a day. Mother worried about this silent child whom she had brought into the world, and wondered if her daughter had the power to assert her own presence on the earth. Where would the mother gather the gifts of speech for her child if it was true that her daughter had lost the gift on that perilous journey out of the womb? The midwife had been scrupulous in the performance of ritual; the child had moved from shadow to shadow, from one darkness into another. Could the midwife have erred unwittingly? Afterwards, she cried, and the women sang her back to sleep, willing a silence onto her. She defied them with her tiny speech-seeking voice and cried all day and all night until the mother fell asleep.

Following the directions of the spirits, the women buried parts of the umbilical cord in different places in the fields, spreading it as though to bless the earth with it. These actions were performed blindly, with no notion of the future. The child's cord, buried in the earth, bound her to the future in ways that she could not revoke. Taking by the neck the small calabash filled with strong-smelling herbs, the midwife followed the ritual of birth, sneezing violently as she went about her task. The mother rose from the mat and sprayed clear white milk from her breast onto the forehead of the newborn, and then over the rest of her body.

For the stipulated three days and nights, the mother and child stayed close together in the darkness of the hut with the midwife. Only the constantly burning fire intruded on their privacy.

Finally, the midwife went out into the world but did not break the circle of time: she refused to shake hands with the people she met. Instead, she went into the forest and dug tubers with her bare hands which she brought into the hut to burn over the glowing embers. The thick smoke from the fire made the mother sneeze but also brought strength back to her body. The rich smoke diffused the persistent smell of cow-dung that had united the women during their wait. When Mother finally went outside the hut, the midwife swept the ground ahead of her with her right hand using a broom made of dry grass; with her left hand she beat ululations that thanked the spirits which had looked after them all. Then she dipped and stirred the end of the broom into a calabash that she held by the rim between her fingers, then raised clouds of dust as she swept. The broom greeted the ground with rapid celebratory strokes.

Before passing the child to the father for the naming ceremony, Mother held her up to the sun.

4

She shouts to the top of the trees, and the birds, in a sudden flapping of wings, fly off in unison into the bushes ahead. They descend together on a bare thorn bush, and wait. She runs, singing, raising tiny clouds of dust around her feet. Her shadow disappears, and she turns, whirling. She sees her shadow swallowed by the sun. She swings the empty water gourd up to her head, and the gourd catches the air on its path and echoes some wild hollow sound that frightens her. The wind sends a cloud of dust billowing across her path.

She stands still beside the road, her face turned to the blue sky, and feels her eyes fill with tears, and her heart rises beneath her. She is dizzy with her whirling, and the ground raises her up to meet the clouds, and she laughs at the sky and at her tears, and at the earth moving beneath her bare feet. Then everything is still, and her feet feel light as she lifts them off the ground, carrying her once more along the path, freeing her. She holds the water gourd under her arm, and it feels solid and round and smooth, pushed against her ribs. Her fingers curve over the rim, holding it firmly in place.

There is no one else on the path to the river. She does not like to meet strangers. What about the story that Vatete had told her about the strangers who stole a child and placed her in a large goatskin bag, ". . . they tied her legs with soft bark and stuffed her mouth with leaves. Then they walked for many days to a faraway land. The girl listened to them talk whenever they sat down to rest but she could not understand the language that they spoke. The girl sang a song taught to her by her mother and put the men to sleep. She freed herself by chewing off the skin of the bag . . ."

Nehanda can hear the rushing river. The lulling sound tells her where the river is deep and treacherous, the fast rippling gurgles tell her of the rapids over which it freely tumbles, and that muffled thudding is the water parting around the large rocks cutting across its width, which is where the people cross to the opposite bank. When she gets too close to the river the different sounds strangely merge and she can no longer distinguish its different parts; the river is almost peaceful. She kneels down cautiously on the bank to collect water using her gourd, and begins by skimming the surface and then using a small amount of water to rinse the inside of her vessel. Afterwards, she starts by pressing her vessel downward into the water and rotating the bottom so that all the floating particles disperse, and when the water clears she dips her gourd and brings it up full. She feels the water run cold over her hands.

The silence surrounding the forest is frightening. The trees reflected in the water ripple and look squashed to half their size. The place is so still that Nehanda folds her legs beneath her feet and digs them into the sandy wet bank, tears rising helplessly to her eyes. She would like to forget that story Vatete told her.

A large black shadow passes slowly over her head and she trembles and wipes the tears from her eyes. The sun has hidden behind a menacing cloud, in friendship with the sky, and that makes her more frightened. Sometimes the sky is not very kind to her. It scares her with the shadows it sends to the ground. Nehanda shuffles backwards, the inside of her toes welcoming between them the grains of sand which always feel largest near the river. She retreats until she is almost hidden by a small thorny bush. She sits silently, curled, her tiny fingers clammy, waiting for the consuming darkness in her head to disappear. Sharp thorns prick one side of her arm as she leans too close to the bush which claims its space for itself. She wishes she had not come to the river today.

Sometimes she sees her reflection in the river and then feels her heart beat violently. The river distorts her image so completely that she thinks it would destroy her also, dissolving her into itself. During such times she almost drops her pot from her trembling hands and moves back suspiciously, away from the enticing water. She likes to watch herself in parts of the river that are still, but sometimes the sun disappears suddenly the way it has done this afternoon, and takes her with it. Nehanda turns around, frightened at the sudden disappearance, which for a fleeting moment is like a vanishing of herself. It is amazing what things make one long for Mother.

Mother assures her that one day she will be so grown up that she will not fear anything. Nehanda sees her future self like a shadow that has somehow separated from her. When an eagle passes high in the sky, the shadow on the ground, many distances from where the bird flies, seems to be no part of the bird. Her own shadow never moves that far away from her; it always remains a part of herself. Yet, there is this other self that Mother tells her about, a self that both of them have not met, not really, but which looks at both of them from the future.

In future, she will be tall enough to get *matamba* fruit from a tree without having to throw large stones at it for half the day in order to bring it down. The fruit always explodes on the hard earth, the smooth brown surface cracking like dry clay and surrendering to the ground the thick brown liquid in which the sweet seeds of the fruit swim. Nehanda rests her hands on the ground, her legs stretched before her; the earth pushes freely between her fingers. Her body begins to feel cramped, and the cold attacks her feet. Nehanda remembers vaguely that she has promised Mother to be back early, but she would rather finish the story about the stolen girl which she had been telling herself on the way to the river. It is not easy to tell a story on the way home when you are carrying a load of water on your head. Some of it spills and runs disrespectfully all the way down your back, even finding its way down your leg.

Nehanda is in the half light of Vatete's hut, listening to the tale, which only a while ago made her feel abandoned. Nehanda chews the goatskin, securing her freedom, frightened.

The strange tongue of the stranger is silenced as she escapes the traveller's bag and wanders through the forest, calling to the hills. She calls the names of her people who propel her feet over the ancient ground.

Nehanda sees the clouds gather into a darkness and descend towards her, and she picks up her water gourd to start for home. The darkness pursues her, seeking her out. Nehanda lifts her small water gourd carefully to the top of her head, her hands trembling. As usual when there is no one to help her lift the vessel to her head, water spills from the pot onto her shoulder. The feel of the cold water frightens her.

She is alert to the sound of her own footsteps as she moves. The grass touches her legs and more water spills out of the pot, going over her face. She wipes it off with her left hand. Her right hand supports her vessel. She walks faster along the narrow path, desperate to get home, irritated by the grass she feels sweeping against her legs.

She hears the birds calling, protesting the gathering clouds, but does not see them chase after each other in the rapidly closing air. Their shadows, however, die along her path.

5

The hut was made of sturdy *musasa* poles dug deep into the ground by the men, then plastered liberally with mud by the women. Long thick grass bundled tightly together with strong bark from the *mopani* had been spread evenly to form the roof. Long poles had been joined to support the thatching. The women had carefully selected and cut the grass from near the river, bringing it in thick, heavy bundles balanced on their heads. Trailing behind their mothers, the children had laughed at the strange shadows on the ground as the women followed each other home. The men had performed the cumbersome task of thatching. It only took a day. The day was made even shorter by a calabash constantly passed around, filled with home-brewed beer. Often a woman had crept out timidly from one of the huts where smoke formed a welcoming embrace around the peaked grass roof, and, kneeling humbly at a distance, inquired if the calabash was still full.

Mother works alone at the entrance of the hut, covering the pillars with cow-dung, protecting them from ants. Her hands reach into the wooden bowl, and the thin consistency runs between her cupped fingers, leaving a curious trail along her arms. Her arms move slowly along the wall. She breathes the green cattle smell.

Mother has not had good dreams since her daughter was born. Her fears began with the naming ceremony.

The women who had attended the birth of the child led the way into the caves, leaving the group of men standing among the prickly cactuses. Mother feels tired as she follows. She cannot hear anything distinctly. She is surrounded by murmurs. Murmurs rise from the earth. She does not like this day, yet it should be the greatest day for her daughter.

Last night, she had dreamt of rain. There is no water, only

feathers.

Black feathers fall from the sky and bury her daughter. She runs through the village asking for help, but no one hears her. She runs through the feathers, which grow around her until she is completely lost, and can no longer find her child. She moves desperately through the thunder, surrounded by mysteries. The rain falls through her eyes. She wakes up in a sweat, screaming, and calling for her daughter. What kind of dream was that to have the night before the naming of one's child?

The women emerged from the caves carrying clay pots, which they had deposited there in the early morning, before the first rays of the sun, in rituals that excluded the men. The group gathered into two circles. The inner circle was made up of the women. Father stood in the middle with the child in his arms, facing the sun. He took the soil he had gathered from beneath a rock earlier that morning, in a ritual that excluded the women. He called to the ancestors that protected his lineage, and thanked them. He mixed the soil with the water in the black clay pot that had been handed to him by the women. He gave drops of the water to the child to drink, and combined her with the soil.

"May you be an offspring of the earth," he muttered. He gave the child more water to drink. The women clapped their hands in celebration. Their hands were cupped, and their clapping was like the sound of their voices.

"They say the strongest tree is one that grows from beneath a rock." He poured some of the water on to a rock. Then he made an imprint on the ground, by holding down the child's foot. "May you find anchor on the earth." The rest of the water, which was mixed with the soil, and in which dead leaves floated, was poured over the child's body.

Mother sees the birds fly off the trees and disappear into the shadows of the tall anthills. Mother is very afraid for her daughter, whom she feels will not be with her long.

17

Then Father lifted the child to the bright sun, which received her with glistening rays, and the women asked the ancestors to protect the child.

"Bind the child to the mystery of the earth."
"May the darkness of the sky bring her rest."
"May the light of the sky bring her wisdom."
"May the sun rise, and set, in her arms."

Mother looks at the sky, and remembering her dream, she is afraid.

When all the ceremonies of birth have been performed, the child's name can now be pronounced without fear. Mother stays in the forest, till the sun has set, before returning to the village. A star falls from the sky on to her feet, turning into water.

Since the naming ceremony, her fear has stayed with her. Mother moves a distance from the mud wall, to look at the work she has completed. She feels no joy, though she has not erred in her task. The empty wooden bowl held beneath her arm, Mother walks into the darkness of the hut.

6

The wind leads to the dead part of the living, slowly searching. The wind pushes dry leaves against the hut.

"There was a long drought. The rotting wind was more than we could bear. The cattle had died in our kraals. We chewed bitter-tasting roots to keep the wind from utterly destroying us. We went to pray for rain under the big tree, walking in friendship with our lengthening shadows."

The child sees Vatete's hands tremble. Black soot floats from the grass roof.

"We walked through the air which carried the current of a dead thing. For many days we walked to get to the tree of rain, many days. Our shadows were longer than we had seen them before, and we sought forgiveness from the sun. The earth opened and received the living.

"We saw the strangers as we approached the big tree. On our heads we carried large baskets full of well-prepared food that we were going to leave at the base of the tree. The tree had a wide trunk. It was older than any living person in the village. There was an entrance into the interior of the tree which faced the direction of some rocks. However, only those who had been chosen by the great spirit that we prayed to could be allowed inside."

The wind circles the hut. The child feels fear form inside her as she listens. "For four days we were supposed to leave food at the foot of the tree. We were there to worship and praise our great ancestors so that we would have rain. Where had we erred? We had not left the mouths of our sacred caves unguarded, without proper sacrifice. Always, we had sent greetings to the earth."

Vatete pauses in her telling, and it is as though she has arrived at a place of rest in the middle of a long journey. Half-burnt wood from last night's fire is scattered around the dead hearth. A bundle of grass for sweeping the ashes, worn to a size that hardly extends the length of one's hand, has been thrown carelessly to one side of the room. An old hoe with a broken handle, which Vatete used in the fields only last year, rests against the wall near the entrance of the hut. Some dried vegetables are kept in an open basket at the *huva*, along with pieces of dry meat.

"When a man appears in our midst carrying breasts on his chest, we do not ask him questions. We know he is a masked spirit and gather to watch him dance. We saw the strangers sitting at the base of the tree. We had never seen such desecration. They had made a fire there and were eating the food they had

19

prepared. Immediately, we withdrew and hid in the woods, but they had heard the sound of our feet on the dry grass. One of them came toward us."

"Were you afraid? I would not have been afraid," the child says emphatically.

The wind has passed on to other distances and left the leaves gathered in a heap behind the wall.

"We were not afraid for our lives. What were our lives compared to the survival of the earth on which we stood? No, we did not fear death. After what we had seen, we preferred death. If they had killed us, we would not have to be the bearers of such disturbing news to our village. Where would we find the mouth with which to tell what we had to tell? It is a hard thing to see strangers on your land. It is even harder to find a stranger dancing on your sacred ground. What mouth can carry a sight such as that? We were afraid only of our ancestors who had been offended. How would we cleanse the soil?"

"What did you say to them?"

"We did not speak to them. We were certain that they had come for gold. Therefore we believed they would not stay, that they would go away after they had done with digging. Because one has gathered the tallest trees from the forest, does not mean one will build a home. The strangers cared only for the wealth of the forest. For a long time we watched them dig. They were scattered through the land, and even asked our men to help them dig for gold."

She drinks a little from the *hari* that the child hands to her. With shaking hands she places the pot beside her bed, and some of the water spills prophecies to the ground.

"Why did the strangers stay then, if they could not find what they wanted. Why did they stay if they failed to find the gold?"

"Often we say that the mouth is like a wounded tree, it will heal itself. But there were no answers to satisfy our asking.

The stranger had come to us on a long journey, and his kin had forgotten him."

"You did not have any rain that year then?"

"The wind led to the dead part of the living. The ground was hard as rock, and yielded no crop. The sun had fallen from the sky. The wind burst into our midst but it gave birth to nothing. It had arrived only to mock us, and carried our death on its back. The strangers, who were digging all over the land without proper sacrifice, had offended our ancestors. We sent sacrifices on their behalf to appease our ancestors, but there was no path prepared for them. We walked in wisdom with our shadows, in search of the dead part of ourselves, which would be our shelter."

Again Vatete receives the clay pot. The child keeps her hands above the pot. When Vatete has secured the pot, the child lets her hands fall. Immediately, the pot drops to the floor. Water creeps slowly toward the hearth. The child picks up the ash-covered broom and sweeps the water, along with the fragments of the earth-pot, away from the grass mat where Vatete lies.

"We did not dream, because we had no sight with which to feed our dreams. Then a millipede moved across the earth, though there had been no rain. In the black sand, it left a soft trail that led behind a rock."

The darkness gathers through the entrance of the hut.

7

Rocks leap out of the fields like a new crop, dotting the landscape. A rock breaks open and sends out life in the form of a small green bush, which also greets one like a spirit.

Mother pulls groundnuts out of small mounds of earth, sending clods flying over her stooping shoulders, and piling the groundnut bushes to create a small hill. Their bristly roots spring protestingly from the ground and stand in firm tendrils. It is as though the roots have been surprised in their sleep. Later, she will snap the nuts expertly from the roots where they dangle in tight clusters, and carry them home in a basket, balanced on her head. Most of the bushes mock her with empty roots. There is not much to harvest. Mother wipes the sweat from her forehead with the back of her hand; she throws the barren bushes into a separate hill away from her.

During the growing season when the maize grows dense and tall and green, it is not possible to see the rocks, yet one is suddenly upon them while weeding the mounds around the stalks.

"The people in the village, haunted by ugly spirits, surrender them to the rocks. There they live in dreadful agony until they can find a human companion." Mother's voice is low and trembling. She does not want to awaken any evil which might suddenly spring upon them, unseen. Mother's legs are covered with the red soil from the fields.

Nehanda rests her hand on her shoulder, close to the string of red beads that goes round her neck, circling her. Her arms, like Mother's, are covered in the red earth. They sit together, the fields rolling behind them with short bushes of drying groundnut held in small disappearing mounds. Nehanda, seeking to gain praise from Mother, has collected a sizeable amount of wood from the adjacent forest to carry home for the evening fire. The bundle rests against a peaked granite rock which casts a truncated shadow over their faces.

"Why do you cry, Mother?" She asks curiously, and sits close to the woman who has already half-filled the basket with groundnuts.

"The earth is in my eyes. It is the earth, my daughter. Come. Sit very close to me, and I shall look at you." The woman pauses in her work.

"Let me help you, Mother." Nehanda drops her arm from

Mother's shoulders, and works along with her.

As they work, the earth creeps up their legs. Nehanda attempts to rub away the red earth covering her legs with her hands, then employs the groundnut leaves which Mother has discarded. She manages to remove the red earth from her arms.

"What is a *mudzimu*?" the child asks her mother, suddenly. The woman moves closer to her daughter, but continues with her work. She speaks slowly, and the air is silent around them.

"Whatever you do, you must not offend your *mudzimu*, or those of others. If you do, many problems will result. A *mudzimu* is like a shadow. It follows you wherever you go. Everyone has a *mudzimu* because everyone has a shadow. Each of us is looked after by a *mudzimu*. But we must also look after them. That is why we brew beer and pour it to the ground, to appease and thank our *mudzimu*."

As she speaks, Mother forces the roots out by sliding a closed hand down the small stem of the groundnut plant. Her motions are quick and practised. She throws the groundnuts into the basket without even looking up. The pile of discarded bushes continues to grow.

"The dead are not dead. They are always around us, protecting us. There is no living person who is stronger than the departed. When the whole village prays together, they pray to the ancestral *mudzimu* of their clan. When we pray to a *mhondoro* for rain, we are praying to the guardian that unites the whole clan. This is one of the strongest spirits of the land."

The shadows from the trees and rocks grow long around them. Nehanda gets up quickly from the ground and gathers the wood she has collected. Using some more lengths of wet bark, she tightens the bundle of wood so that she can balance it easily on the top of her head. With some small groundnut plants, she also makes a ring which will go on top of her head to form a cushion between herself and the wood. She makes a tight knot that holds the wood together. Beneath her right arm Mother carries the basket filled with the groundnuts she has harvested, and they walk from the fields till they enter a path in the forest that leads home, their shadows following unseen behind them. The air carries the sound of escaping wings.

Nehanda feels the sun set in crimson ripples behind her.

8

Smoke billows out in thick clouds through the small entrances of the cooking huts. As the children watch, those who emerge from the huts are transformed into spirits, the smoke wrapping around their bodies in grey clouds, and rising over their heads and arms in ghostly trails. Lighter than air, the women move in circular motions that lead back into the huts, swallowed by the smoke. The clouds are like ash thrown into the air and carried by the wind. Voices rise into the sky with the smoke, thin and vanishing.

A clique of selected men, young and newly married, move behind the huts and slaughter a cow chosen the previous day. Soon large pots, filled to the brim with meat, are placed over big roaring fires. Toothless grandmothers, though incapacitated by age, ululate around the fires. The younger aunts elbow each other with knowing messages and raised eyebrows that say, "We will have to boil the meat into a porridge before everyone will enjoy it."

The celebrations follow the completion of all rituals pertaining to the new year. None of the food will be eaten until all the proper rituals have been performed to the satisfaction of the presiding spiritual leaders who are the eldest and most respected leaders of the clan. They collect a sample of each crop from what has been harvested and, kneeling under a *muhacha* or fig tree, appeal for a blessing.

Those women who have given birth during the year bring their children, now already crawling and walking, to be named anew and blessed. Those who are trying to conceive, or have lost their offspring in repeated still-births, also come to partake in the rites; they hope for the transforming power that comes from time without beginning, from the ancient sources of fertility.

Neighbours forgive each other their disputes, and are seen exchanging basins filled to the brim with food. The older women who are the designated peace-keepers wink happily at the reconciliation that, earlier, they had failed to bring about. The atmosphere holds everyone in conciliating laughter. The sacred presences protect the earth.

Across the yard the children run after each other in animated play. One of the masked presences gestures threateningly toward them, and they scatter away like seeds, breaking into anxious laughter, tumbling over each other, shrieking, sending the birds flying over the trees, then resting in the long waving grass.

The spirit is an old man with a stoop, weighed down by a bag which contains secrets of the forest. He has been walking since the day he was born, without rest. He is the strongest man in the village. But the children laugh at his stooping body. He has never slept and therefore knows all the animals of the day, as well as all the animals of the night. "What is your name? What is your name?" The children are ready to rush away when he threatens.

"My name is One-with-the-name-that-cannot-be-said-in-the-daytime."

"My name is One-who-refuses-to-sleep-and-listens-to-hooting-owls."

"My name is One-who-lost-the-goat."

Then the spirit takes a wooden mask out of his bag, and wears it above his masked face. Silent, he sits at the edge of the clearing. He refuses to speak. The children, too, are silent. He is so still behind the mask, some of the children whisper that perhaps the sleep he has lost since he was born has finally arrived. Tired from their excitement, the children sit quietly within the clearing, watching. They listen to the enormous silence of the mask.

Nehanda, however, has been sullen all day. She sits behind her father's hut, her back against the mud wall. When Mother returns from the river, she is surprised to find Nehanda still sitting there, her eyes focused blankly into the distance. "Are you going to sit there till the sun has gone to its mother?"

Nehanda sobs. Her hand soon spreads the tears down her neck and across her forehead. "Those birds in the air. Do you see them? They have come from beyond the edge of the earth.

"We ask you to arrive well among us." Nehanda points to the sky.

"Nehanda! Nehanda!" Mother shakes the child frantically, to wake her from the dream that would carry the child away. "Where are you going? Are you dreaming?"

"Who are you?" Nehanda asks.

"Close your eyes, my daughter." Mother keeps her hands on the child's shoulders, detaining her from journeying into territories from which she might not return.

"The birds, Mother, there are the birds. The birds are flying freely without their bodies. The large swooping wings disappear and the bodies of the birds return and they are naked without any wings or feathers. Look, the black crows have returned to the sky. There are black crows in the sky, so many of them that they block the sun from the earth." Nehanda raises her arm.

"What shall I do?" Mother's plea is directed to those beneath the earth.

"Is it night, Mother? I cannot remember . . . , tell me, Mother. Tell me of that which has come from the sky."

"Where are you, you inhabitants of the ground?" Mother asks, and beats the ground with her fists.

Nehanda covers her eyes with her arms and lies still on the ground, her throat dry with weeping. "There are crows in the sky . . ."

Two older women plead with her to get up, but she defies them. "Leave me . . . !" she screams desperately, as though her life is threatened. She kicks dust into their faces. She spreads a bit of saliva across her arm and sees blood in it.

Soon she is asleep, and is carried into the hut. Mother sits alone at the edge of the dancing ground. She has not had any peace since the birth of her daughter. The feathers have come like rain, smothering her. The time with her daughter will be brief. No. It is only a dream.

Mother runs through the village, calling for help. Falling. She is falling from a great height in the sky. Her voice lingers but no one will hear her. She has fallen to the ground, her voice wrapped around her. The dancers raise dust to their knees, and she can no longer see through their legs. The dust swells, threatening, and she moves back. But it lingers, in circles, indifferent to her fear. Mother closes her eyes as tears move down her face. The dust settles suddenly over her legs. The dust is cold on her feet. Horrible, this fear that pursues her.

The young men dance and capture the attention of the maidens, but Mother thinks of her child who sleeps alone in the hut.

The *mbira* players who sit in the inside of the circle of spectators send quivering mournful sounds through the air, reminding one of birth, of death and of the serene presences

of the departed. The *mbira* is the sound of water falling on rock, and of water flowing along secret and diverse streams. It is the weeping of those who inhabit the earth. Mother feels the water move over her shoulders.

Meanwhile, the *ngoma* players pound the skin of their drums relentlessly and send young men leaping in fine contortions into the air. Some of the most revered musicians of the village are present. Each of them plays not only for those present, but also for the departed.

If Mother had the gift of sight, she would see her daughter in the clouds of dust that the men raise around them. Nehanda has not missed the celebration, though Mother thinks her in the hut. Nehanda sees all the activities, and dances on the shoulders of the best dancers among those gathered. The dancers stamp the ground valiantly. The spectators who stand in a circle cheer and sing, their feet covered in dust.

9

The beetle creeps along the dead riverbed in silence, rolling the past before it, and survives. Nehanda holds her silence all day, offering it with the palm of her hand as though it were something solid. She shouts. Though nothing can be heard from her, she wails until she brings herself to deafness, until she has closed out the earthly sounds that try to penetrate and disturb her silence. Meanwhile, the spirits perform prophetic dances on the ground before her, and send deafening echoes through the ground.

A lizard disappears into the crack along the mud wall of the cooking hut, chased by a hen and its young with wings flapping. When the prey has been lost, the hen pecks the ground angrily. Scratching the ground rapidly with its feet, the hen disappears into a tiny cloud of dust and the offspring move away in fright.

The women rise before the men to make the morning fires and prepare food. A woman who slept till the sun went into her mouth would be considered incapable of raising her household. Nehanda, who sits on a mat behind the hut, does not notice any of this activity. She sits with her legs stretched in front of her, and her arms folded across her chest, but often she releases them into her lap. She had woken before the first rays of the sun.

Across from where Nehanda sits, Mother is pounding maize, using a long pestle. The ground thuds with the sound of her effort. Mother, grown far beyond the age where she could lift the heavy pestle with ease, now pounds the grain in slow ponderous motions. Her movements are so slow that she could say all the praise names of her lineage within the time it took her to raise the pestle and then bring it into the mortar.

Time has brought changes that are borne out by the sagging skin below Mother's arms, by the wrinkles around her elbows, the crest of white hair on her head, the pronounced stoop, and the continual muttering. She talks constantly, even to the wind and her shadow.

The chickens pick at the white grains which fly out of the mortar, but when they get too close, the women shoo them away with hands covered in flour. Sometimes they throw a small stone at the chickens, which disperse in every direction, veering toward the rolling object just in case it is something edible.

Mother stops in her labour with the long pestle held still between her hands. Her eyes are hidden under the tired skin which falls from below her eyebrows, almost blinding her. Tears run down her cheeks as the wind passes. Mother turns with difficulty to look at her daughter, and after much thought, she proceeds with the work, muttering to herself. No crisis is sufficient to make the men go a whole day without nourishment, not even death.

The chickens, unable to pick anything more from the maize that has now been pounded into a smooth consistency, approach a plate of cooked *nyimo* that Mother has put down. They are almost at the plate when Mother sends them flying and clucking in all directions. She shoos the chickens away, accusing them of treachery against her world. Brown and black feathers are left scattered on the ground, some flying on to the mat where Nehanda sits, and soon the chickens are pecking busily for bits of seed behind the *hozi*, a small raised hut where the food provisions are stored. Nehanda is oblivious to the commotion her mother has raised.

In her desperate silence Nehanda longs for a new language to seek wisdom, and new ways of seeing. She has banished the sun from her presence.

Nehanda keeps her eyes held tightly shut during the day, until the edges of her cheeks hurt, and the darkness surrounds her. The darkness spreads along the horizon, filling the earth. She sees the redness beneath her eyelids and is reminded of the treachery of the sun. The sun has sent a cloud of locusts which has transformed day into night.

No words come out of her mouth but she speaks with an ever-increasing desperation. She rocks back and forth, but no one hears her invocation. She speaks with the guidance of the departed which shape her tongue into words. Words grow like grass from her tongue.

Nehanda waits in the darkness for the masked presence that will tell her of the long night that has been sent to the earth, and of the moon that sits rotting in the heavens. The light of the heavens has been stolen from the eyes of her people, and only the fires give them warmth, when they can once again find each other's faces. Only the scarred faces of her people tell them they have been in battle. They are shocked at this transformation of their bodies because they cannot remember the call for battle. On which plateau has the battle been fought, and against which adversary? Surely they have not fought one another?

The distances are now hidden by the darkness, and they cannot see into the future, or into the past. They are trapped in the moment of their abandonment. The departed surround her with promises of birth. Caught in the moment of birth she sees time move like water into the future. The water falls gently from the sky. The water falls on dead rock. It is herself. Nothing surprises her and she sits motionless, her eyes unseeing. The spirits sit cross-legged across from her, revealing distances to her spirit.

"The darkness has gathered."

Though she does not respond, she hears a voice that answers.

"Indeed it is dark, but it has been dark for a long time. We are in the season of night. It has been night since morning. The sun has vanished from the sky. We bear the marks of the moon on our faces.

"Something has passed over our heads. Beware of trickery. Yes, some trickery is in the blindness rendered through words. Beware of blinding words!" Her shoulders shake as though with cold, and her arms tremble. A shudder passes through her body, and she points to the sky, and the horizon circles the earth with crimson cloud.

10

The *dare*, or village gathering place, is marked off by vertical poles, and reeds tied together to keep the wind out. Within the shelter is a circle of stones on which visitors sit, with another circle of smaller stones at the centre, where a fire can be made on cold days. A calabash of ancestral beer has been placed here. In the outermost circle, the women can be heard whispering. From inside the shelter, only their heads can be seen rising above the long poles. The children find gaps between the poles through which they hear the guarded voices of their fathers.

Ibwe raises his voice above the impatient murmurs. "The elders delivered our message well. The white man treated our elders with contempt. He had no respect for what we had to say. The stranger was told that our ancestors are not pleased with the presence of the white men. He laughed at our elders and our beliefs."

The calabash is passed around the circle of gathered elders, and each takes a sip. They watch as Ibwe's shoulders and neck become hunched into a more forward posture. His stomach protrudes, and his arms hang oddly. He takes a few awkward, plodding steps, and when someone laughs, his aggressive stare makes the audience shrink back. His eyes are those of a dog that has not yet decided whether to attack or to run away. His jaw has moved forward, so that the words, when he continues speaking, seem to force their way out of his mouth. The people understand that the white man is now standing before them.

. . . "I will give you guns, and teach you to pray to my God. He will strengthen you, and give you victory over your enemies. The things you believe are not true. Your ancestors cannot help you. My God is the only true God. He will bring you peace, wealth, and happiness."

Ibwe pauses again, the people see the white man depart. "Our elders insisted on their message. They spoke without anger. They spoke not with their voices, but with the voices of the people. He did not listen to the voices that were sent to him. He held his gun as they spoke, mistrusting them. 'We come in peace,' they said. 'We ask you to leave our land and our children.' He looked at them as though they were children, without respect.

"Our elders spat on the ground with anger, and left without farewell. It was good that they had brought their walking sticks, for the ground beneath them shook. The white man will not leave this land willingly. Our elders say that the stomach of a stranger is like a small horn, it cannot empty your granary." Ibwe acts the role of a humble stranger respectfully receiving food.

Then again he begins to transform himself. Placing both hands on his prominent belly and opening his mouth slightly wider than before, he plods slowly round the circular space. Before a word has been spoken, the people have understood that the white man is not a humble stranger. He looks at his hand, which holds a piece of paper.

. . . "I shall read everything to you, and you will see that it is very clear. I am a messenger of the Queen. The Queen is like your *Mwari*. She protects, and wishes to extend her protection over you. I shall give you guns with which to fight your enemies. In return my people will be allowed to search for gold. You can trust me."

The white man departs, and Ibwe transforms himself anew. Although he is a short man, the people see a tall man standing before them, majestic in bearing. He carries a staff which he waves ceremoniously to decorate his speech. When Ibwe continues speaking, it is in the voice of their own chief.

"Our people know the power of words. It is because of this that they desire to have words continuously spoken and kept alive. We do not believe that words can become independent of the speech that bore them, of the humans who controlled and gave birth to them. Can words exchanged today on this clearing surrounded by waving grass become like a child left to be brought up by strangers? Words surrendered to the stranger, like the abandoned child, will become alien—a stranger to our tongues.

"The paper is the stranger's own peculiar custom. Among ourselves, speech is not like rock. Words cannot be taken from the people who create them. People are their words."

The chief nods as he hears his own words being spoken. He bears proud marks on his forehead, and on his legs. These signs, which the stranger views only as scars, are the marks that distinguish him. Sometimes he bears other signs that are less permanent, painted for particular rituals and festivities. He can even invent signs that will immediately be understood by his people as his own. Indeed, these signs help to communicate sacred messages among the people. Though the chief knows all these signs, he does not want to betray them to the stranger.

Ibwe pauses to drink from the calabash. Then he hunches his body, plods his way across the circle, plants his feet firmly in front of the chief, brings his face close to the chief's face, and stares pointedly at the marks the chief bears. Shocked, the people draw in their breath audibly, and murmur in surprise at the insult. Ibwe waits until absolute silence has returned, then forces the stranger's words out very slowly.

"Do you have your own symbol?"

A chorus of exclamations rises from the gathering. Some shake their heads with laughter, while others raise their voices in anger.

"Put your mark on this paper. Any mark that is yours. Do not use any symbol that is shared by others. Do you have your own symbol? Can you make a mark like this?" Ibwe picks up a twig and marks the earth in a childish manner.

Then he turns and stands tall, in a posture of dignity.

"There is no man that lives among other men who has his own animal. We are all born together. Thus do I know who is related to me."

The voice of Ibwe moves slowly through the assembly, uninterrupted, and reaches the women who respond with song and incantation.

"The words of the stranger are plentiful like grain. Locusts fill the sky with sound. The visit of the stranger has made night longer than day.

"The smothering smell of cattle rotting in the field reminds us of our loss. Where is the bull that carries the name of our grandfather? Where is the bull that carries the name of our grandmother? In the river we watched the water turn to stone. Mistrusting the sky, birds have died along the path to the river.

"The first grave-digger washes his hands with muddy water and the rest pour ancestral waters over their legs. The eldest son is given the name of his father, and the departed protect and guide us. The departed no longer witness our ceremonies of death. The departed are filled with forgetting.

"A seed lies at the bottom of the dead leaves, nesting life, waiting for the rain. But the sun has moved to the edges of the earth. For how many moons shall the stranger be among us?"

The voices of the women move sorrowfully among the men, beseeching. The children accompany the voices of their mothers with clapping. The men listen to the women, who continue to assert their presence with muted song. One of the men stands up and speaks. The custom is that each one should be heard.

"Our elders have taught us the power of words. Words must be kept alive. They must always be spoken. The white man wishes to remain a stranger to us. It is not only important that a man speaks with words, it is also important what gestures he uses for his argument. The stranger has refused to sit among us."

Another of the men stands to speak. He has to shout to be heard in the growing agitation. He even raises his shield into the air, to arrest the attention of those around him.

"We allow him to dig for gold, but the land is not his. The land cannot be owned. We cannot give him any land because the land does not belong to the living. While we live, he is only a stranger here." When he has finished speaking he waits to hear what others have to impart.

"Has he heard us? He must remember our argument. We have said it with our mouths, and he must listen. We wish to talk again."

"He says he has spoken. He carries his words in his palms, between his fingers. His words tremble with the wind."

"We will not surrender our words onto the side of a calabash which a child may break one morning. He has said that our words will last beyond several moons. Does he not know that there are other words for the future, plentiful like seeds?"

"How can words be made still, without turning into silence?"

"Silence is more to be feared than the agitation of voices."

"Indeed, the stranger has unusual customs."

"The white man held the paper like a sacred thing. His hands shook, and we mistrusted him."

Some of them laugh at the foolishness of the stranger. Others express anxiety. A man wearing a headband stands up. In the wind, its long red feathers seem to reflect his turmoil.

"For how many moons will the stranger be among us?"

The calabash is passed around the circle of gathered elders. As they drink, Ibwe lifts his arms towards the sky, as though the answer to this question will be delivered to him. The women again raise their voices.

"We cannot remember how far we have walked. We cannot recall which proverb we once uttered to lead us into the future. Shadows melt into the earth. The sun has swallowed the earth. The wind whirls and waits. The wind leads us to the

36

dead part of the living.

"For how many moons will the stranger be among us?"

11

One feels the heat so early in the day in Africa, Mr Browning thinks. He can hear his servant, Moses, moving about in the next room. Moses had once told Mr Browning his heathen name, but Mr Browning can see no point in using it. The new name is easier to remember, and more importantly, it is a step toward the goal of civilizing the country. Like the embryonic garden outside Mr Browning's window, the name creates a space in which Mr Browning can feel comfortable. Moses does not yet seem to understand much of what represents progress, but Mr Browning is confident that his efforts will bear fruit.

"Moses! Moses!" He shouts as though Moses were many miles away. How is one to get prompt action from Africans if one does not shout? Moses comes in bearing a white metal bowl of water and a white towel draped over his left arm. A cake of green soap is placed on the edge of the bowl, which is flat and wide. While Moses stands very stiffly in the centre of the room, Mr Browning dips the soap into the water and proceeds to wash his face. Some of the soapy water splashes onto Moses's uniform; and he will have to change it. Moses closes his eyes against the droplets, but does not move. He keeps his eyes closed until Mr Browning has stopped splashing. "You can open your eyes now, Moses," Mr Browning says. What a fool this Moses is, a real clown. He wonders what his wife will think of Moses. His habits are embarrassing.

What a fool Mr Browning is, Mashoko thinks. He places a china plate on the table directly in front of the chair that Mr Browning will occupy to consume his breakfast. Just beyond the plate and slightly to the right, he places a saucer containing a teacup. Then he carefully sets down a knife, exactly two inches to the left of the plate, and a fork and spoon, precisely two inches to the right of the plate. Having completed his inspection of the garden, Mr Browning re-enters the house. His eyes are wrinkled, and small moist patches have already appeared below each of his armpits; later, a much larger one will spread across his back. Mashoko tries to avoid looking at him.

Mashoko does not find his work interesting; in fact, when he is in his village he feels ashamed of it. If it were not for the hut-taxes that he is being made to pay, he would not accept the work. His cattle will be confiscated if he fails to pay the money asked of him.

Mr Browning sits stiffly on the straightbacked wooden chair. Mashoko stands behind him and to the right, holding a pot of freshly brewed tea, its spout breathing on a small patch of bare skin on top of Mr Browning's head. Mashoko steps forward and directs a stream of liquid into the teacup. Then he places the teapot in the middle of the table. At this moment, Mr Browning's fleshy fingers touch the knife and the fork. "Moses, how many times must I tell you, you must put the fork on the left side of the plate and the knife on the right. You get it wrong every day. Look, man, fork, see this, fork on left, knife on right. You must try to learn this before Mrs Browning arrives.

"Look here, don't look over there while I'm talking to you." Mr Browning stands up and waves the instruments in the air. "Knife on left, fork on right. No! dammit, that's wrong—knife on right, fork on left. Shall I set it to music and sing it to you? Lucky for you I have the patience of Job, otherwise I would have sent you off long ago."

Mashoko walks proudly into the kitchen, and flops the eggs from the pan onto Mr Browning's plate. Then he carries the plate of food into the other room where Mr Browning is holding his teacup in front of him. All of the fingers of Mr Browning's chubby right hand are pinched together at the tiny handle of the cup, but only three of them are actually touching it. Mashoko places the plate in front of Mr Browning. In his own compound, Mashoko has a woman to bring his food to him. Mrs Browning will arrive soon, but Mashoko does not think that she will be preparing Mr Browning's food. Someone, either Mashoko or someone else, will wait on both of them.

Afterwards, he stands at the corner of the room, and watches Mr Browning eat. Mashoko is convinced that Mr Browning came out of his mother's stomach with his legs to the sun. "Moses, a glass of milk," Mr Browning says, without lifting his eyes from the plate. Mashoko walks to the table, and moves the milk to a place beside the empty cup.

12

Caterpillars grow wings only through death, rising in bright glowing wings, only to prepare for another death.

"Is it not said that we cannot know how the sun shall appear to our eyes tomorrow because we have not seen it? Mother interrupts the women in their speech, and they wait, the pestles held in mid-air. "We do not know what the future brings. Let us respect her silence. Let my daughter be. Perhaps that which wishes to be part of her will not allow her to marry. She is a woman, is she not? She is industrious, is she not? She has ancestors, and a lineage, and totems that she respects, does she not? Is it not enough? What is our power against the seasons, against the wishes of the departed?"

Mother silences the women effectively. Some intervene with commonplace words, which dwindle into apologetic coughs and smiles and gestures, but she pays no heed to them.

A lot of drink and food has been prepared for the people who will be helping plough the soil and plant the new crop.

Long after the women have left, Mother sits mumbling to herself, her head supported by the palm of her hand.

"She has been sitting on that mat for so long. She has not even greeted any of us."

"She is indeed strange. If she does not get married soon what will happen to her?"

"A woman who stays unmarried will be troubled. A mother cannot tell a daughter to get married, that is why we have to talk to her."

"She is headstrong. I would not dare talk to her about such matters."

"Do you think she can still bear children? As long as a woman is not married, she will be talked about as if she were a young girl, even if she has already lost half her teeth."

Mother mutters angrily, the voices of the women crowding her. Amid the voices she sees a cloud of dust move around her, burying her pestle which lies abandoned on the ground. The soil gathers around it, and it is completely hidden. Mother is agonized. Her head moves back and forth. Though she tries, she cannot move her limbs to save her pestle. Her shoulders are heavy with sleep. The red soil climbs over her feet, rising to her knees. She has lost her daughter, whom she has watched over for so long. The mat on which Nehanda has sat all morning is empty. It has been rolled away and rests against the wall of the cooking hut. Nehanda has departed into a darkness from which she will not return. Mother falls to the ground, digging for her pestle. She must find it. The dust protests in blinding clouds. Mother digs the ground with her bare hands, but she can no longer find what she seeks.

When she finally opens her eyes, Mother finds the pestle resting safely between her hands

* * *

Mother walks a long distance to arrive at the village of her kin. She carries heavy words of a silence she can no longer bear. She walks slowly. Her walking is her dreaming. Her feet carry her without triumph through the burdened air. She sings of birth and death. She sings of the ash that has fallen from the sky.

"My daughter is not my daughter," she tells her assembled relatives with tears streaming down her eyes. "My daughter is not my daughter."

"What has she done, has she said anything to her mother that her mother finds hard to forgive?"

"My daughter is no longer my daughter."

She looks down to the ground, and weeps.

* * *

The *n'anga* arrives with his goatskin bag bulging with a variety of medicines. He wears a mass of animal skins, including a high hat, full of white and red feathers, whose band is made out of leopard skin. Some of his most potent medicine is carried in an ivory horn, which dangles on a tight rope of skin, from his goatskin bag. After accepting a hen, a goat, and other valuable gifts, the *n'anga* undertakes the task of confirming the identity of the spirit that troubles Nehanda.

His ankles ring with circles of dried tree seeds. As he walks into the yard, he asks the women to sweep his footprints from the ground behind him. All of his orders are obeyed. He unrolls a mat on the ground. He has brought the mat tucked under his arm. He sits close to Nehanda and watches her curiously.

Circling his wrists are small wooden animal carvings tied closely together with a thin black cloth. After he has laid a variety of bones on the mat in front of him, he closes his eyes. The bones have been taken from different animals in the forest. Lions, snakes, the small wings of birds. His collection of divining bones, or *hakata*, are the most important articles of

41

his occupation. He regroups the bones and gathers them into his hands, then casts them randomly to the ground.

His head shakes vigorously, to indicate the weight of the task. He takes some medicine from his horn, and spills it in a circle around the bones, then he casts them again. He pauses, and takes some time to read them. It is clear that a spirit intends to manifest itself in Nehanda. He identifies it as a good spirit, and insists that the people should welcome it with a feast. The spirit will be a great help to the people, he says.

The *n'anga* breaks into song, then goes to the back of the cattle-pen. When he returns the people have found another gift for him, which he accepts. He sits down again, then asks for water. When he has received the basin, he scatters into it some of the medicine from his bag. He dips his staff into the water, and then rises from the mat. He proceeds to sprinkle the water around the huts, to prepare the ground for the day when the spirit will be welcomed into the person it has chosen.

Nehanda sees her shadow move searchingly across the earth.

13

The government station that Mr Browning has built on the hill is thriving. He now has ten African policemen. He has given each of them a bicycle and a uniform to distinguish them from the rest of the villagers. He has also taught them to put authority in their step by walking stiffly, their shoulders raised to the sky.

Mr Browning walks around the house to pass the time, as is his habit. A letter is on the writing desk near his bedroom window, and Mr Browning fights a growing impulse to re-read it. Even as he walks outside the house, his thoughts are really inside the building, and he can clearly see the contents of the house and of the letter, which he has already read many times. This is not the first letter Cecilia has written to say that she is coming. Mr Browning chooses to believe her this time.

By midday the sun will be unbearable. Mr Browning can already anticipate the anxiety that overcomes him at such times. The sun's rays penetrate the eyes so that one walks about in blindness.

"Mr Browning . . . Mr Browning . . . Mr Smith is here." Moses speaks from a distance. Because he stands so far away, and because he really does not want to raise his voice, he appears nervous. His lack of confidence does not endear him to Mr Browning.

Mr Browning does not answer, but turns around and walks back the same way he has come. He goes past Moses without looking at him. Mr Browning's mind is already on Mr Smith. Often he comes home from the office in the late afternoon and meets with Mr Smith, his junior. Sometimes they tire of each other's company and of each other's voices. Then they just sit on the veranda and look at the stars, and the darkness. Sometimes they each find a book on the shelf to read. Mr Browning wishes he had brought a larger library to Africa.

Mr Browning sits uneasily on the edge of the chair. He is a short man. A round squat frame makes him self-conscious when in the company of taller, more solid men, like Mr Smith. He holds his lips tightly as though to hold off some statement of self-dislike. Even when he speaks, he does not relax, but seems engaged in the most strenuous struggle with his emotions. This feeling, reflected on his countenance, does not

disappear even when something chances to amuse him.

"Smith, do you know the difference between us and the natives? The difference is that we know where we are and the native does not."

"Surely the Africans know the land . . ." Mr Smith answers dispassionately.

"I mean the knowledge of the world that we have. We have drawn maps, and know how to locate ourselves on the globe. The native only knows where he is standing. I have been collecting maps since I was a boy. This is what we should teach at the new school, a knowledge of the earth." He taps the table with his fingers.

"Maps. The native. Hmm . . ." Mr Smith looks amused, then continues. "What is the use of showing, um . . . paper . . . to an African?"

"It is simply a consciousness of the world, and of one's self and one's place in it." Mr Browning's voice is filled with conviction.

"Map-reading? Hmm . . ." Smith is amused, and laughs.

Mr Browning abruptly turns away from him.

"The African must begin to go somewhere. He must be given a goal in the future." He is talking to himself.

"I sometimes wonder why I have stayed in Africa so long, although it is a fairly appealing place. One can easily stand outside things," Mr Smith says, breaking the brief silence, slowly nodding his head.

"Action is progress." Mr Browning speaks between clenched teeth. Any meeting of these two men was always a commingling of passion and indifference, leaving both of them resentful.

When Mr Browning continues, his tone is curt. "You should get three of the policemen from the station to take you around the villages. We should build the school close to the village," Mr Browning says.

"Goals are constricting. I value my freedom. Freedom

emanates from nature itself. It is the charm of Africa that ideals coincide so perfectly with nature."

Mr Browning moves his chair further away from Mr Smith.

Mr Smith does not know why he bothers to visit Mr Browning. Perhaps he is not indifferent to the sound of an English voice.

Mr Browning rises from his chair and walks to the edge of the veranda. He flings out his short arms, as though to encompass the whole of Africa.

"Have you spoken to the villagers? They have not taken well to the missionaries on the other side of the village. Reverend Thomas came to tell me that they had burnt down the church. You will have to go there tomorrow afternoon, and see what can be done." Mr Browning speaks from the edge of the veranda.

"Missionaries . . . missionaries . . . What do I have in common with men who plan for a future beyond the earth?"

When Smith continues, it is to ask Mr Browning about his plans for the school. "How will you persuade parents to let their children attend the school?"

"The natives will soon see reason. The villagers only sent old men to persuade us to leave. They believe I can bring this about. They refused to understand anything that I had to say. Everything will take time." Mr Browning congratulates himself on his resolve not to pursue the matter with the village elders, although a further action from himself would be completely justified. It incenses him to witness Mr Smith's indifference at such close quarters.

Both men look into the distance and wait. "It seems natural to keep one's eyes focused on the distance in Africa," Mr Smith says. "The landscape appears monotonous since the horizon is always before one's eyes, without any distracting landmarks to obscure vision. The foreigner in Africa is always in a state of waiting; the horizon turns one into a dreamer."

45

Mr Smith has chosen to be in Africa in the interm until another impulse arrives that will lead him away.

Mr Browning suggests moving their chairs into the shade. Mr Smith complies. All of Africa is the same to him. "Moses! Moses!" Mr Browning shouts in the direction of the door. "We would like some tea?"

Moses responds without delay, bringing a tray. As he lays the items on the table, Mr Browning and Mr Smith resume their conversation. "I shall introduce order and culture," Mr Browning says, as Moses pours the milk into his tea and Mr Smith extends his cup to be filled. "We should enlarge the prison," Mr Browning continues. "We need order and justice."

"Natives . . . black policemen . . . they do not like each other," Mr Smith says.

"Every Englishman has a proper sense of justice, and we can more readily execute the duties of our office with the assistance of native policemen. When left to arbitrate over their own quarrels, the natives can spend days at it, losing much time that could be invested in labour. We shall teach them the most gainful use of their time." Mr Browning's voice is precise, knowing.

"They do not like being imprisoned," Mr Smith says. He watches Moses pouring the tea, and this activity absorbs him much more than the conversation. Behind the two men, red-flowered bushes throw a translucent glow over the surroundings.

Large red hibiscus petals burst and yellow dust gathers over them. Pollen and nectar surrender their sweetness to the heated air, inviting birds and bees. The bees wander uncertainly into the bushes, hovering with outstretched forelegs in ritual dances over the fertile ground.

Mr Smith strikes at the mosquitoes that land on his bare arms; his arms are soon spotted with smudges of blood.

"Are you collecting insects again this afternoon?" Mr Browning asks him.

Mr Smith spent many hours walking about in the forest,

and always he found some insect that he had not encountered before. It was as though each new insect he saw had somehow deliberately eluded him, for why had he not seen it until this time? He took prisoner any insect that he found, and was fascinated by, and put it in one of the small bottles that he always carried with him. He avoided putting two species together, and when he ran out of bottles he might put a specimen in one of his many pockets. There the insect might be forgotten, and gradually torn to pieces. In the evening after he had had his dinner, he would sit beneath his lamp, and remove the wings and legs from his insects, examining their size and coloration. He would examine the eyes and antennae. When he cared to, he scribbled a few notes in his diary. During his stay in Africa, he had devoted a lot of time to its insects.

14

A man emerges from the crowd carrying a long horn which he blows in song. His feet accompany his actions with dance, and the crowd breaks into clapping as he re-enacts a hunt. His face bears courage, and the people urge him on. The man has long hair that straggles down his face in knots, and his skin shines. His face and actions are charismatic, and he pulls the people's eyes to him and they watch the familiar hunt, and wait. He has come to the gathering with a particular message, but he, too, waits.

Some of the dancers are wearing *magosho* around their ankles, and these rattle as they stamp their feet on the ground. The women are ululating and clapping. The voices of the women are raised in song. The *mbira* players send powerful rhythms through the deep sounds of the drums. The stretched skin of the drum releases a frenzy of dance from the young, but the old are incapacitated and watch from the fringes of the circle.

The drum brings no edifying messages, and the young who play upon it do not know what messages they can send into the future. They call out the names of the clan and of their lineage. The dust rises from beneath their feet while Nehanda sits at the centre of the circle, oblivious to the activity around her. Her head sways, too heavy for her. Her face is motionless and placid, bearing no signs of the agitation within her. When her eyelids lift, her face dances. Her shoulders rise in height, while her arms grope the air.

A woman wails desperately and collapses on the mat. Other women lift her into the hut, where she is attended to. Encouraged by these signs, the men clap their hands and play vigorously on the drums, while the dust moves around their feet which the dew had visited early that morning.

Shadows lengthen but the dancers, clad in short animal skins wrapped around their waists, find strength to keep their feet in the rhythm of their invocation. Their faces are painted with clay. Circles are drawn on their foreheads, and gashes spread across their cheeks.

A large calabash, filled with herbs, is brought and placed on the ground near Nehanda. A woman sweeps the ground within the circle of dancers, then dips her broom into the calabash, following the well-known cleansing rituals of her people. She sprays the water over Nehanda while the crowd respond with deep chants that speak of their hope for the future.

She shakes her head. The earth below her resounds with the pounding of feet. The cloud of dust circling her brings tears to her eyes. Her voice comes out in spurts, and what she says cannot at first be understood. The people deafen themselves with song.

Beneath closed eyelids she can detect the redness of the sun, and those to whom the story is told sing to accompany the story-teller. Their voices move as though from an infinite distance.

"Is this how it happened?" they ask. "Will it be such a future?"

The leader among them dips the branch in the clay pot and beats the ground with vigorous strokes.

* * *

"Was that the sound of the owl in the distance? What sound was that?" Nehanda asks, seeking assistance from the air with frantic motions. Tears flow from beneath closed eyelids.

"That is *Shirichena*," they say. "That is the bird of light."

They cup their hands together and clap in unison. "Tell us . . . tell us . . . you who have been sent from beyond. Tell us . . . you who have seen the secrets of the departed. Help us find ourselves."

With blinding feathers *Shirichena* guides them into the distances from which their future is told. It soars over the tops of the hills, and into the yellowing horizons where the mist has settled to greet the treetops. "This is where it all began." The voice speaks of the beginning of the world. "Those who travel long journeys shall not be abandoned by the spirits, or be left to sleep in the grooves of tree-trunks." The leafy branch sends drops of water across her forehead, and the darkness departs.

"Here in this desperate valley where the grass was once green I hear the birth of voices. It is hard and convulsive, like other births. The green valley is a place that holds hope and warmth. At the bottom of the hill, and then at the summit of the hill, not only would I see the wonders and trials of a past time, but even I would be transformed."

When she has fully opened her eyes, Nehanda rises slowly from the ground where she has sat for so long, moving slowly as though her body aches or is too heavy for her. Her brow now carries furrows, knitted in anger. She has aged dramatically, as though overnight she has inherited the wisdom of all her departed. At these signs the crowd continues to sing as though to teach her the meaning in her voice, encouraging her to speak. Her body breaks into spasms and her face bears the pain of her struggle. After a long and desperate wailing, Nehanda points in the direction of the hill, and stamps her feet on the ground: it is the hill that had been the first to be taken by the settlers. Again she lets out a sound that begins as a shout of joy but recedes into a cry of agony. Her quivering voice tells of fear and suffering.

"The valley was spacious and surrounded by mountains covered with lush grass. From the mountains, rivulets flowed filling a small lake in the fertile valley in which fishes of various kinds swam. The valley, however, is no longer green with birth. Its grass is dry, and the sediment of memory swallows boulders of grief." A murmuring confirms the tale to be told.

"You too have been chosen to tell this story, to accompany the story-teller on the journey which may not be embarked upon alone. The story-teller needs an accompanying tongue.

"The vibrating air is not all I feel and hear; the voice of the departed is borne upon the dancing arrows of the morning sun. The green leaf once again hangs upon my forehead." The people listen and accompany her with song. "I see vultures!" she shouts into the sky, her pointed finger moving across the sky. "There are vultures in the air!"

She turns around and points to the hill once again, and she keeps her eyes focused there. The tears in her eyes form deep rippling horizons. "We were not prepared for such a long journey. We did not think we could live long enough to witness an arrival. Still, we prayed. Our heavy feet sought the rain but did not find it. Reluctantly, we witnessed the slow invasion of the land.

"Our eyes sought comfort, but the sky accused us of neglect. Empty enclosures replaced our ancient claim. Our ancestors say they have been abandoned, and when we worship, our voices can no longer reach them.

"We extended too long a hand to the stranger. Now there is much work to be done, and it must be done quickly. Together, with our spears and our hard work we must send the enemy out of our midst . . ."

The crowd retreats from her, respecting her command of the ground, her territorial claims. The people listen to the voice of their ancestors. They listen to the unmasking of their destiny. Their song changes to agony. They too feel the warm rays of the sun, and the white shadows are in their midst. She spreads the words like water over their heads, and they bow down before her. The children who had been playing in the distant trees, stop and sit in the shade. There is a shift in their belief and in what they hope to discover in the new day.

"I am among you. I carry the message of retribution. The land must be cleansed with your blood. You must fight for what belongs to us, and for your departed. I will speak until the birds depart from the trees."

She tells them what those who had gone before have said, and what the future holds for them. They are in agony as they listen, afraid to hear of where they have erred. As always, they grant authority and privilege to the departed. They look to themselves first for any failing, and do not always blame their ancestors. Their ancestors only punish them if they have over-looked their duties to the dead.

Nehanda's trembling voice reaches them as though coming from some distant past, some sacred territory in their imagin-

ings. It is an alluring voice, undulating, carrying the current of a roar that reminds them of who they have been in the past, but it is also the comforting voice of a woman, of their mothers whom they trust. Her voice throws them into the future, and she speaks as though they have already triumphed, as though they only looked back at their present sorrow. But again she abandons that voice and brings them back into their present sorrow.

The crowd recognizes and salutes the spirit medium that has been sent to them for the sake of their relief. They are pleased because this means they have not been entirely abandoned. It has been long since they have sorrowed at the arrival of the stranger in their land.

The men stop dancing and kneel around Nehanda, and the women in the outer circle cast protective shadows over the bending bodies of the men. Nehanda closes her eyes and speaks with a trembling and troubled voice. Her voice rises higher, as though to reach every crag surrounding the village. Her voice carries the heart-breaking tender cry of a mother for a lost child.

"We have dug dead roots from the thirsting soil, tubers that mock us with fists of dry rot. The forest in which we have hunted has become a land of diggers. The ground echoes, echoes. We saw ungodly guns gathered near a bush, and we made our retreat. Touching them with terrified shaking fingers, we fought the fierce anger in our hearts.

"From the tree flew predictions in the form of birds that we had not seen before. They soared over our grey heads and were quickly swallowed into the cavernous sky. The oldest among us beat the ground with their sticks."

She pauses and listens to the lilting sound of the *mbira* which permeates her whole body as she moves gently back and forth. The *mbira* moves in circles around her and she follows its weeping with her shoulders. A shadow guides her to a place beneath the earth where she sees her own death. She breaks into terrifying screams. The *mbira* continues to weep. When she recovers Nehanda sends more messages to the people.

The people clap their hands in unison, showing their submission to Nehanda's spirit and truth. It has been a long wait. Now the truth is among them, and they succumb. The truth has reached them circuitously. It is not easy to see the truth when there is so much dust in the air.

"The dead are not gone. The dead are among us, guiding us to clearings in the future where we shall all triumph.

"Our ears are full of sand and insects, which together make such loud and disturbing noises that we are completely lost.

"Voices sit on the branchless trees and call out to us with a multitude of sounds that have travelled long distances through the heated air. We called and called to our ancestors until our voices vanished into the threatening sky, but we continued with the raspy grating on our throats—the soundless calling into the air, but still we were not delivered.

"The water falls over our heads, and down our necks, leaving cold paths that remind us of death. We were alive, and dead with hopeless longing and prayer.

"The rain was brief, though we thought for a while that this would be our relief. Was it another sign? We chose not to contemplate, and sat on the rocks desiring forgetfulness, desiring sleep.

"Frantically, we beat on the tight skin of our drums and hoped to be heard. Soon the honoured and eldest among us put away their drums, and resolved to wait: a voice was needed, a promise.

"The messages in our silences needed to be witnessed. We needed more than our physical strength, we needed our old selves and clarity."

Her face is held to the sun, still and unmoving. Her eyes glisten with the sun's rays. She has kept her eyes open to the sun, her face raised in a gesture of challenge to the sky. She speaks directly to the sun, as though it carries a greater memory than her own. She reminds the sun of how it has abandoned the earth. Nehanda turns around and picks up the broom that has been left near the calabash at the centre of the circle. She dips it in the calabash and sends water into the air, stamping her feet in song.

The water streams down the side of her arm as she waves the broom in the air. She walks around frenziedly, and then stands quite still. After gazing at the crowd which follows her eyes, she speaks again.

"Countless days, unlike any we had seen, went by. Each dead draining day delivered us into unknown turmoil. Our trees no longer bore fruit, and we dug the earth fruitlessly. From the top of leafless *musasa* trees we watched the strangers disperse into the forest. When we spoke they could not hear us, and we were like children to them. They walked freely, and we were sure that they felt the land was already theirs.

"Explosions rose from tongues that defied our understanding, and voices came whispering from the past, but the messages were unclear and we failed to decipher them.

"Even in the silence, sometimes we were sure something vital to our future was communicated to us, but we could not hear what it was. The spirits too had adopted a strange tongue that we could not comprehend."

Her eyes are animated with the new life within her, and they burn with the agony of their task. "Where will you be after you have been disinherited? You will be forgotten beneath the earth.

"I see a timeless cloud of dust that will blind us all, and we shall never recover from it."

Once again the water with her accompanying words falls like rain over the people, and she dips the broom into the calabash. Soon her calabash is empty, and she turns it upside down, and places it at the centre of the circle in front of her feet. Because it is now empty the calabash echoes the silence of the crowd, and their desolation. Her trembling voice comes among them again, and it carries with it her tears, which now roll freely down her cheeks. A calabash has broken in her eyes.

"Is this what our ancestors prepared us for? Did they prepare us for a death among thorns? Do you already feel shame to claim what is yours? Do not submit to the unknown wisdom of strange tongues. Those who have submitted to the spirits of the stranger have brought an abomination to the land. Can we defeat an enemy whose god is already in our midst? Rise up, I say. Rise up and fight."

She does not care to hide her tears. She takes the empty echoing calabash once more, and after balancing it on the palm of her hand and running in circles around the enclosure that the crowd has formed around her, she throws it into the air, and the women gasp. When it reaches the ground, it breaks into four segments.

"Spread yourselves through the forest and fight till the stranger decides to leave. Let us fight till the battle is decided. Is death not better than this submission? There is no future till we have regained our lands and our birth. There is only this moment, and we have to fight till we have redeemed ourselves. What is today's work on this land if tomorrow we have to move to a new land? Perhaps we should no longer bury our dead.

"Our dead should not be left to rot on the ground, unburied. Why should we dig graves in empty ritual? In places where we have buried and worshipped, new owners have arrived and led us off with guns. How long shall we suffer this indignity?

"Who are these strangers . . . these gold hunters? Our men helped them hunt for gold, and we thought they would leave. Now they hunt us out of our land. Is it not clear that they have discovered that our land is the gold they sought?"

Outside the circle of singers and dancers, she turns back and speaks once more. "Raise your spears. Move into the mountains, I say. Worship your ancestors. Your ancestors shall protect you when you begin to release yourselves from this bondage.

"We should have shaped our truth out of stone. We should have mounted spears along the borders of our village and thrown spittle into the eyes of strangers. We opened our arms and embraced a cactus bush, and it has brought the desert with it."

When she has left, the horn-blower emerges again out of the crowd. His name is Kaguvi.

15

She weeps in agonizing ritual, and lets her cry and her feet propel her over the stolen earth.

The children run and hide in the huts, away from the woman who walks briskly in a flood of tears. Nehanda turns to face the women, who have now been joined by the men. Her eyes glow with passionate energy, and her voice calls upon them for sacrifices.

She walks twice in a small circle, in a ritual of her belief. The crowd responds with clapping and praise and ululation. Her front skirt, which is made of animal skin, covers her knees. She shouts, searching the distances. "Voices have surrounded us all night. We have sat vigil to the voices that sent arrows to conquer spaces on dead bark. We saw our future carried in the wind.

"We did not heed the pealing laughter of the stranger who did not believe. He had been with us for a long time, but we did not allow his mouth to diminish us. He asked us to kneel down with him and he would teach us to pray to his own dead, but we were not persuaded. How could we pray to the traitorous spirit that had guided him into our midst? Instead, we cast words at him, then sorrow, then spears. He tried to place strange words in our mouths. We discovered bitter words of our own that would stand vigil on our tongues.

"The stranger hated the naked beauty of our dance. We danced around him with spears raised in the air, and he was afraid. We guided him into the shadows, and told him we were going to pray. We did not ask him to pray to our ancestors and our god. We were not so foolish as to offend our spirit with voices from the mouths of strangers. The stranger looked upon our raised spears with scorn.

"At midnight, helped by the stamping of our aching feet, our voices rose together, calling painfully. Our voices trembled, because we were waiting for the past to be among us. The future too was before us, sending arching arrows on dead bark, and we did not know if we were ready for the future to find us. We were not prepared to shelter our shelter-seeking selves.

"The timorous rays of the trembling moon etched their whispers on the black heavens; our toes dug the forgiving earth and burned with rushing blood. We sought the beginning of the world. The air resounded with the speech of our beseeching hands. The earth released a sigh that was only the beginning of speech, and we waited.

"The sigh was a wind-carried cloud of dust that rose around our feet and propelled our frenzied dance. Our eyes tightened in agony. We danced. We heard our feet meet the ground and resound with the beginning of speech. On the fringes of our dancing-ground burnt a great fire.

"In the centre of our circle was placed a rounded calabash filled to the brim with tears. Its mouth was turned to the earth so that those who were below us, whose help we sought, would have no doubt that the calabash carried only our tears. It had been filled with water in the early morning but we poured it on to the ground when the first star adorned the sky."

She turns away suddenly and races up the hill under which

they have been standing. Her cry is so loud and so piercing that the people following and watching her feel their own hearts break. They sing sad mournful tunes that tell of their sorrow.

Some of those who have followed her sit down to rest under the trees. She disappears from view and they hear her cry in the distance behind the thicket of trees and rising granite stones, and again they follow. She walks with firm steps in circles to the top of the hill where she spits on the ground and turns back for her descent. A small wind climbs the hill and meets her on her descent, but she does not turn away from it. In the hills she has traversed with the message of her cry, another wind rises, loud and captivating: the hunter Kaguvi.

16

Spotted locusts leap from beneath the thin and wet leaves of grass where they feed, covered with dew. They greet the day with no knowledge that their lives will be brief. When Kaguvi arrives at a village, it is as though he has emerged from the horizon.

On the first day of his seance, Kaguvi is led to the cattle-pen, where he is blindfolded, then handed a spear. With the spear he smites the bull which he has chosen in his blindness, the sharp weapon sliding soundlessly into the heart of the beast. The bull falls suddenly to the ground, blood spurting in crimson streams into wooden bowls which are brought by ululating women. The blood is life and death. The blood is given to Kaguvi to drink while the men dare him to drink it, and the women challenge him with songs of warriorhood. He does not hesitate. When he has drunk, he runs around the enclosure chanting messages to the departed bull, whose strength he has now inherited. Finally, with his forehead still bearing spots of crimson, he speaks with a faint voice that seems to have travelled distances to arrive.

Kaguvi is humble and beseeching before the people, who are the only ones with the power to grant him authority over their future. Afterwards he roars like a lion, and waits for the heart of the beast to be given to him. Again he does not hesitate; he eats his portion raw, the blood streaming down his arms. The people applaud him, and welcome the ancestors who speak through him.

"Remember our might. Remember the resistance that we showed to the white man when he first arrived, of the contempt we felt for those who had tried to change our lives. The taste of pride will be like drops of honey on our lips."

"My name is Gumboreshumba!" he shouted. "My name is Leg-of-the-lion!" In his death-denying dreams he shapes a meandering path full of secrets that will only be discovered in the next dawn. The power of his evocation is not lost, and the youths carry it away with guns and spears. He speaks for the reshaping of lives.

Now Kaguvi speaks with his dancing staff. He stands in the middle of the circle of people, under the shade of a large *musasa* tree, the largest within two days' journey. The men of the village dance enthusiastically around him while bearing branches which they have torn from the trees. Together with Kaguvi they enact a traditional hunt which speaks of their intention.

Kaguvi would rather beat the drum than shape his message

into words. He shakes his spear in intricate motions in order to demonstrate his purpose. He climbs the trees like a sentinel sending his spear in diagonal paths across the horizon. The people believe in their inevitable triumph, in the beauty of their souls. Kaguvi gazes longingly into the hills.

He raises dust with his pounding feet, until the earth responds with the echo of the chanting feet of his people. With his bare feet he stamps out a trail of ants, following them right to their anthill, then taunting and stamping on those that emerge. When he looks at the people they chant in agreement, their hearts throbbing.

Kaguvi carries the horn always with him, and a staff that he waves in the air. He wears a hat made out of black ostrich feathers. His strength is preserved in a black skin bag which he carries on his back. No one has ever seen its contents: the claws of a lion. During his seances, the villagers relive their lives. Kaguvi dances their hopes into being, dances their future and past triumphs, dances their histories, dances the forest that surrounds them, dances the hills and the plateaus, dances until the sounds of the birds become their own war-songs, dances until the strength of the lion is in their limbs. The flight of the eagle is the speed of their feet, the cry of the jackal surrounds them, and their spirits soar and they dream only of their success.

Voices throughout the forest speak to Kaguvi with waving silvery-bottomed leaves and flaming flowers. Rocks bear the faces of his ancestors, the horizon tells him which path to take to avoid his enemies, the black crow shows him what spaces in the forest will protect and heal him. He borrows messages from the riverbanks where the sharp-edged reeds wave, and the water tumbles over an uneven bed.

The rebellion gathers its own strength. When he closes his eyes, the voice of Nehanda comes to Kaguvi. The voice gives him strength, and he works with it towards achieving the goals of the rebellion. Drummers and runners cross the forest from village to village, spinning a web that will envelop and destroy. Kaguvi waves his staff across the faces of the people and speaks with a reverberating dreamlike voice, and they listen, chanting.

A man emerges out of the crowd bearing his shield, and carries a blood-curdling shout into the circle that the people form around Kaguvi. He wears a ring of red-painted feathers around the crown of animal skin over his head. His face and arms are painted with red clay. He dances to the crowds, affirming the truth that has been spoken, shedding the humiliation he has suffered since the arrival of the white men. He dances well and is soon rewarded with shouts and joyful clapping, which encourage him into more elaborate motion. The man is Mashoko.

17

That day, Mr Browning and Mr Smith talk late into the night, the room illuminated by the fast melting candles held on the table.

"I have heard these people sing every moonlit night as though they are happy. Why have the policemen left without provocation?" Mr Browning is the kind of person who needs to hear himself think.

Moses has left. Mr Browning keeps hearing his voice. "When a stranger arrives among us we give him food and shelter. Where one is surrounded by humans, one cannot perish. I hope you shall always be surrounded by humans." Moses had come to him while he was writing a letter at his table. When he looked up, Mr Browning felt sure he had been standing there for a long time.

"Yesterday I greeted you and stayed, but today I part."

Mr Browning had been surprised to see him wearing his

traditional clothes. He carried his shield under his arm.

"Did you hear the drums last night, and the weeping?" Mr Smith asks, interrupting his thoughts.

"The Africans perform many rituals. How can one account for what strange ritual leads them to their performances? You cannot understand what these natives believe," Mr Browning says in the half light, cursing as the tip of his pen breaks.

"I am proud of my people. I am going back to the wisdom of my people," Moses had said.

Exhausted, Mr Browning puts aside the stack of government papers he has been browsing through. He gets up, stands by the window, and looks out at the night sky. "The natives are rather quiet for such a warm night." The candlelight dies behind him.

Moses had spoken to him with unaccustomed confidence. "The wealth of a man is measured by his cattle, and by the size of his clan. A man is respected and praised because of the strength of his words."

"Is it possible Nehanda has some real sway over these people?" Mr Smith asks, breaking into his thoughts.

"I doubt that the natives can listen to an old woman like her. What can she tell them? This society has no respect for women, whom they treat like children. A woman has nothing to say in the life of the natives. Nothing at all." His voice quivers. Mr Smith maintains his silence.

"It is hard to deal in a civilized manner with people who possess so many superstitions." The urgency of introducing the Bible in Africa had never been more clear to Mr Browning.

Mr Smith likes the sounds of the night insects. The crickets are singing outside, and a bat flies in through the open window. Mr Browning rises to close the window, then looks around for a weapon to use against the offending creature. He has picked up a shoe which he throws at the bat. It swoops around the low roof and lands on the floor. He picks up a book and lunges for it without success. Smith does not even turn around while Mr Browning frantically pursues the air. He shouts, running across the room. Breathless, he perseveres. He will not be defeated by this creature that has intruded into his space. Mr Smith watches with a vain curiousity.

Yes, Africa does have its moments. Mr Smith moves to the end of the room, and stands leaning against the wall, waiting. When it becomes apparent to Mr Browning that he will not succeed, he opens the window, and feels something pass his ear. The bat has fled into the night air unharmed.

"We are a proud people," Moses had said before leaving the house.

Mr Browning curses. Mr Smith returns to his place near the table. The light of the candle brightens his amusement. Mr Browning moves his hand slowly across the flame while his shadow leaps back and forth across the ceiling. The open window sends the curtain flapping against the chair.

* * *

After Smith has been missing for two days, his body is found tied to a fig tree in the middle of the forest. His pockets are filled with dead insects, and his collector's bottle, with a beetle in it, is found not far from where he lies.

The priest sits near the window, keeping his eyes to the sky. Mr Browning paces the room. "Who would have thought these calm placid people would revolt," he says. "The only certain thing is never to trust the natives, no matter how well behaved they seem. They are the most dishonest race on the face of the earth."

"The natives have already killed twelve white men at Nduroma Station," the priest says. "That is only forty kilometres away. The rebellion has already claimed many lives. They are unaccustomed to work, these natives, that is why they are fighting us. They prefer to sit in the sun all day, than to be brought under the most advanced civilization in the world."

"They would have resented any government. If we had been angels they would have stolen our harps. We have to subdue them completely, otherwise they will never learn that the ways of the white men are superior to their heathen beliefs." Mr Browning feels betrayed.

"Only the rifles will Christianize the natives. This Nehanda is a wizard. After all, what more are these kaffirs besides bloodthirsty cattle-keepers?" The priest responds to Mr Browning's shadow which moves across the wall. When it stops, he knows Mr Browning is about to respond.

"We need a search party, especially to rescue our laagered men. Who is this Nehanda, and this Kaguvi?" Mr Browning laughs. The priest keeps his hand on his Bible. Mr Browning carries a knife with which he slashes the air.

"We are a proud people," Moses had said.

18

The grasshoppers hold to the grass with wings made wet by the dew, and they cannot fly. They bite into the stems, waiting for the rays of the sun. While they await the moment of their release, they wave their antennae in search of their future selves.

Nehanda closes her eyes and the darkness descends. The black cloud spreads across the sky, then is torn into shreds, and the rays of the sun spread between it.

Nehanda sits beneath the shadow of a large rock. The rock has a wide base, with several smaller rocks perched precariously on top of it. The shadow spreads in curving shapes around the barren trees. Further on, the trees cast their own curious shadows which pattern the dry grass. A large black cloud moves over the bright sun, and the shadows on the ground disappear. Crows hover above the trees, calling to one another, and their large shadows move over the faces of the people, and pattern the rock on which Nehanda rests. A group of birds fly past together, their path forming one large bird. A struggle takes place up in the tree where a bird nests as an eagle struggles to get food; an egg falls onto the stones. It spreads yellow liquid that soon dries over the rock, dripping to the ground.

Nehanda's eyes are held tightly as she rocks back and forth, listening to the song within. Her legs are folded beneath her body, and her hands are spread over her knees. Reaching to her left, she drinks from a small clay pot holding water from the river. She pours some of the water into her cupped hand and spreads it over her body. Through her back she feels the warmth of the rock against which she rests. Around her, circling voices rise.

The people return from distances that they have travelled, while others depart. All come back to listen to the spirits that have guided them, protected them, sent them on their path, fearless.

"We received the voice of the departed. We followed the voice of the departed. We shall be strengthened by the power of those beneath the earth. We moved through the midst of the strangers, and we were invisible. Look, we have come back whole, having achieved our aim. We have shot arrows through the air, and they have landed. Let it not be said that we did not fight, that we did not execute all the messages of the departed. Like the wind we have swept through the land, attacking every stranger on our path. Meanwhile, they have attacked us with guns, but we have persisted."

The man waves a long spear covered with blood. In his left hand he carries a gun. He kneels on one knee as he sings praises to Nehanda, who has protected him as he moved through the settlements of the strangers. "Tell us great spirit. Shall we survive the retaliation of the stranger?" one man asks, his voice filled with trepidation. He has seen how quickly a man dies from the gun.

"Do not take anything that belongs to the stranger. If you have brought anything that belongs to the stranger, surrender it there beside the entrance to the cave. Take only the guns. If you touch anything else that belongs to him, even the spirits shall be offended. The spirits will abandon you for such a travesty. Take only the things that will also protect you, not the things that will destroy you. The stranger can only bring ruin and evil among us. Do not covet anything of his. Approach the stranger with a single eye, the other should be blind. It is the envying eye that will destroy us, that will change us entirely. We can become stronger and whole if we believe in our own traditions."

More men surround her with their own messages, reporting to her that they had done as she had asked. They have been successful in their attacks.

"The blood of our enemies now flows through the land. May the spirits protect us in this struggle." The men retreat from her, and speak again. "Shall we remain whole after so much bloodshed? We are a peaceful people. Will peace once again return to us?"

The people throw the guns onto a heap at the entrance of the cave. "Protect our feet on the earth. Lead us to a place on the earth from which we can drink, and find promises of the future. Dark clouds surround the top of trees. Shall we find hope in the future? Shall we be released?" The people call with one voice that circles the hills. An echo reaches her from the sky. It is the voice of the departed, which is also themselves.

Abruptly, she gets up from the ground and points in all directions of the land, telling them to follow those directions, and to repeat their actions till the stranger is no longer among them. If they persist, the stranger will certainly depart.

"Our people have fled to the hills. This is where we shall fight our enemies. In the hills we shall protect ourselves from the stranger. Tell us, great spirit. Shall we be successful in the hills?"

"In the hills, the wisdom of the departed will guide you. The past is in the hills. We shall make appropriate sacrifices, and all will be given to us. Do not fear anything. This is our land given to us by the ancestors. Protect it with your blood. The gnarled roots of trees are brothers with the earth. This is the season of journeying to our origins, to the beginning of our beliefs, and of time. This is the season of planting new hope in the ground, and of weeping. This is the season of night, of locusts, and of long shadows that have banished the sun from the earth."

After a time Nehanda opens her eyes, which are filled with prophecies and calls out to the people, "You must continue to fight. You must not rest. Your power shall be granted by the departed who surround you with their spirit."

A big fire is lit in the middle of the clearing surrounding the rock, and dark smoke rises into a cloud that soon spreads above them, blocking the sky. The people listen to Nehanda as she seeks the voice of their ancestors who are among them. The fire burns high into the sky. Nehanda rises, and throws everything into the fire that has been taken from the white men except the guns.

"The tradition of the stranger shall destroy us." Nehanda speaks as she gives guns to the people.

* * *

She goes into the darkness of the cave, and waits. Voices come to her from the earth, entrusting her with messages for her people, urging her. She dreams the futures of her people whom she sees walking in freedom on their ancient ground.

Once again the people return. She stays in the darkness of the cave, and speaks to the people from within, out of their sight. Her voice is that of the departed. It comes from the beginning of time. The people stand at the mouth of the cave, calling, asking her to pass to them the voices of the departed.

The voices tell of the battles that they have fought.

The voice comes from within them, from the cave, from below the earth, and from the roots of trees. The voice awakens the dead part of themselves, and they walk with new beliefs, with renewed wisdom. Purged of their fears, they are prepared to live and to die.

Her fingers are alive within the clay pot, surrounded by the cleansing water from which she draws the secret of her survival. She seeks the beginning of time, which is without beginning. She seeks the will of the departed, and their strength. She seeks the wisdom of the elders, which has never left the earth.

If she does not wrestle triumphantly this night, her people will be utterly destroyed. In the solid darkness surrounding her, she feels something grow. It gathers, growing steadily out of the rough walls, scurrying across the floor of the cave. She responds frantically, walking bent, in circles, under the low roof of the cave. A heaviness grows on her shoulders, and she crumples to the floor, cursing.

The floor of the cave is covered with small stones which she feels push below her body. She lies on the ground and the smell of the earth fills her, and gives her strength. On the opposite side of the cave, hovering above her in the darkness, sits a large bird. She does not see it, yet she can feel its presence. Its eyes move over her body, waiting to destroy her. Then she hears the flapping of heavy wings, and the air inside moves. She listens intently for the bird to move once more, so that she will know where to direct her scorn. The spirits are with her, shielding her against ruin. She hears claws scraping the ground, and sand flying against the walls. She opens her eyes and seeks the animal, but it is one with the darkness. She hears it move again, and she knows that it has flown out of the cave, into the night. She sits upright holding the clay pot between her fingers; it is now empty. Her voice rises from within her and goes round the room, searching.

"We danced the future into our midst. We danced our past, and our dance was also wisdom, and a conquest of our former selves. The torrential rain beat the earth, digging furrows in which flowed our tears. The tears tore portions of ourselves and carried away our faults. They flowed with the blood of our enemies.

"We danced our sacred dances, desiring forgiveness from the departed. The clouded sky burst into flame and the red earth resounded with our feet. Below the burning clouds the rain fell in torrents.

"We stood in amazement along the dead dry banks of the river where we had gathered. It held no sign to remind us of the previous rain. There was no sign of the flood we had witnessed. The sky was caked with mud, which held big boulders from a forgotten life: it had been a partner to our deception.

"Tree roots pointed to the sky, still and unwavering. We preferred the aberration of dream to this sterile reality. We longed for the murmuring motion of the rising river which had reminded us of birth, and growth, and the promise of our relief. With anger we moved the boulders out of the riverbed and threw them into gaping grooves in the forest, and waited.

19

Only a few gnarled trees are anchored in the soil and the lightning seems very close overhead. Large roots climb over massive rocks which, defiant, perch precariously on smaller rocks. The rocks are steep-sided and form protective enclaves where herd boys shelter from the storm, and where they retreat in search of the ancient spaces of their initiation, in brave celebrations that give promises of their release.

While the path seems clear overhead, and the openness of the flat hilltop is inviting, the obstacles toward the top are immense. The hills are filled with silence. The silence echoes the wisdom of the ancestors, and the presence of *Mwari*, who has put the strange rocks on the earth. One hill is more remarkable than the others. The creator of the hills may have formed it first and used it as a stool. Or perhaps it was created last, for it seems almost perfect. The top of the stool is like a woman's hands cupped to receive secrets from the departed. The elders say that once, on the death of *mhondoro*, a great spirit of the land, water was seen flowing from those hands. At the bottom of the hill, the water was swallowed up by the earth. The earth trembled to receive the departed.

On all sides the summit of the hill is protected by a near-vertical slope, except for a narrow passage, a steep defile, which leads straight up one side. People have spent several days collecting rocks of various sizes, and struggling to alter the positions of certain large boulders. All day the surrounding country is surveyed from vantage points on each side of the hill, while most of the people remain near the top of the ravine. At night the people sleep in a large cave just below the height, but at no time are all of them asleep. The trees and rocks rise in dense and defiant shadows.

Late in the afternoon, by whistling a pre-arranged signal, one of the lookouts conveys the message that men are approaching on horseback. The news is given to the people, who position themselves along the edge of the precipice above the narrow passage. A few of the people are visible from below, but most of them remain just out of sight.

The men on horseback approach in a long, dusty line, squinting into the sun. All of them carry guns, and a man at the front of the column has a sabre, which he uses for pointing. Five men remain behind in a group, their horses facing in different directions. The tail of each horse swishes occasionally.

The man with the sabre leads the body of men toward the ravine. There is an abrupt transition as each horse steps from the scorching sunlight into the gloomy passage. Here the air is clammy, and it feels much cooler. Water trickles from the mossy face of the rock, and in places the ground is soft underfoot. The horses snort at the sudden change. They continue to sweat as they struggle up the steep slope, but now their sweat does not dry, and they begin to shiver. The men urge their horses on with soft words. One of the horses slips to its knees on the wet rock, and cries out in protest. Its rider dismounts and leads his horse on foot. Others follow his example.

Halfway up the slope there is a place where rock has fallen. As a result the passage has been so narrowed that only one horse can pass at a time, and then only with difficulty. From a position directly above this obstacle, a man peers over the edge of the precipice. His face is covered by a screen of leaves, and he remains motionless. He observes that in the gloom below, the last few of the approaching men have stopped just below the narrow place.

The rays of the sun are now horizontal. The man with the sabre, who continues to lead the column, is the only one who has not dismounted during the ascent. He pauses as he approaches the final and steepest section of the climb. His horse, already able to scent the drier air above, paws the ground, eager to leave the dank shadows. Looking up, the man notices that a star has become visible. Rigel? Strange, for a moment he thought that rock on the cliff-edge just behind him had moved. Long day, hard climb, trick of light. Not Rigel, he thinks. Probably Sirius.

The first three boulders fall almost simultaneously. An egg-shaped one is propelled by three women, one pushing the top while the others use a log as a lever. It lands just behind the man with the sabre, striking nothing on impact but achieving a remarkable roll, injuring two horses before coming to rest at the narrow place halfway down the hill.

A larger, more angular boulder is launched by knocking away a log on which it has been propped. It lands directly on the hindquarters of a horse, which is soon afterward shot by the man who had been leading it. This rock rolls only a short distance and comes to a rest.

The largest boulder is about as high as a ten-year-old boy, round on one side and flat on the other. It is pushed towards the sun over the precipice by eight men. It bounces off the opposite wall of the cliff, then again off the opposite wall just above the ground. It does not strike anything directly, and breaks into two pieces upon impact. The smaller of the pieces remains at that point, while the larger one rolls towards the obstruction and lodges in the opening, constricting it further.

A hail of smaller stones depart into the air, whirling. The smaller boys and girls throw first-sized rocks, while the men and women hurl boulders as large as a person's head. The first throw is difficult to accomplish. Larger rocks cannot be aimed, but are sent over the edge by one or more people pushing with their feet of by using logs.

On the slope below, confusion is general. Horses rear up, their eyes bulging; a few of them plunge recklessly down the slope. Some of the men attempt to take cover behind a horse or a rock, in order to use their guns; however, with the attack coming from above, this move is not very effective. Others attempt to retreat down the hill, where they find the constriction now blocked by injured horses as well as by a continuous flow of rocks. A few of the men, including the man with the sabre, continue to struggle up the slope. At the top they encounter two guns; a meagre arsenal augmented throughout the battle by captured weapons.

Some of the captured guns are carried back along the precipice to the strategic point, and are discharged into the melée below. By now nightfall is complete and retreat is manifest. The bombardment is halted and nine men with spears and six guns creep down the slope to acquire more weapons. In the morning a tally shows that at least fourteen men have been killed, and eleven rifles captured. Some other men have undoubtedly been carried away. Seven horses have also been killed and two captured. None of the people has been injured.

The people sing as they descend from the hill. The warriors hold their spears above their heads in praise of the ancestors who have seen them safely through the fight. Kneeling on the ground, they clap their cupped hands in celebration of their strength, and the strength of their people. The elders among them shape the appropriate words to the departed, asking them to continue looking after the people.

"Do not abandon us in this fight," they cry. The others clap their hands again, and speak. The sound of their clapping fills the forest with song. "The words have been given to you. Yes, we ask you to protect and shelter us. You are the ones who can see where the eye cannot see. Therefore, protect us from our enemies." To protect their memory and their hope, they raise their shields into the air.

They return again to Nehanda from whom they seek inspiration and wisdom. Though they have survived this attack, it is clear to them that it will not be long before they too have to surrender with the rest of their people, and go back to their villages. If not, their kind will certainly perish from the earth through the guns of the white men. Their victories during this fight have been many, but not enough to ensure their safety. They will only be safe if the white men leave the land.

When they arrive at the clearing where they have previously consulted with Nehanda, and where they are meant to see her again, she is not to be found. They call into the mouth of the cave, clapping their hands to show respect. The cave answers with silence. They wait long in hopes that she will return to them. Perhaps she is walking through the forest. The loss of Nehanda would mean the loss of their link with the departed. It would mean death.

It is as though they have been utterly destroyed. Around the cave, they see footsteps of the white men.

The signs of the white man's presence send fear through their hearts. The footprints have gone round their sacred ground, which is no longer sacred after this abomination by the strangers. They wonder if it will be possible to restore their link with the departed after so much transgression. Their voices rise with their spears into the empty air.

After much deliberation, and asking the spirits to protect them, the people decide to enter the cave to see for themselves if Nehanda has been killed. They clap their hands respectfully as they bow their heads under the low entrance, avoiding the jagged edges of the rock.

There is not even a clay pot to be found.

20

The spider weaves silence out of patience. Sending spindly legs into the future, it weaves all of time into its hungering belly. The sun sends rays through the spider's disappearing feet, and the air dare not move. There is no relief to the spider's trickery, only a trail of bloodied saliva, death woven into a ball of dust. The spider satisfies itself with slow speed and quickening wit, with full belly and mocking laughter. The spider moves gently through the insect-filled air. Weaving riddles into the air, the spider claims its space from branch to branch, in the armpit of the solid trunk.

Nehanda walks through the forest absorbing chaos out of the empty air. She brings out words with a lashing tongue, for those who are confronted with challenges too hard to bear can only defend themselves with speech. She knocks words out of the sheltering rocks. Silence is made speech, to flow commingled with fate-transforming words. She, who has dared to speak will not be found with an idle tongue, but she will change even the seasons of humankind. The threat of the white men follows persistently on her trail, but she is at home in this orbit full of welcoming ancient secret spaces. She is determined to outwit her pursuers.

She has already outwitted them, casting gloom on their triumphant pursuit. The forest receives her, while those who follow her pollute it with evil footsteps that would destroy her and her people. She spits angrily into the bushes, hating her pursuers with a tormented passion, crying as she feels her strength ebb, her eyesight dim, while sounds of gunshot haunt the hills behind her. The smoke from the white men's fires tarnishes the horizon.

A loose black cloth hangs over her shoulder, and falls over the rest of her body. Half the cloth is damp with sweat, so that the moisture sucks the thin gauze-like material until it sticks to her. When she moves fast through the tall dry sheltering grass, the wind carries her garment to her face, but she hardly notices. The green treetops rise like green clouds rolling at dizzying speeds ahead of her so that she pauses, her hand against her hips, her tongue wetting her dry lower lip, and the air bursting out of her body in retching coughs that seek to weaken her. Afterward she throws herself onto the grass full of briers, lying prostrate until she feels her blood flow less maddeningly through her limbs, and vision return to her eyes. The mist clears, and the green treetops emerge from the fog.

From the ground where she now sits with her feet in the stream, Nehanda watches a chameleon try to cross the water using an overhanging branch. As the chameleon nears the end of the branch, it weakens and dips slightly into the stream, forcing the chameleon to withdraw. Its movements are slow and patient. After a while it tries again. Its tail curls over the branch. When it dips downwards, the chameleon hangs on patiently until the branch reaches the ground on the other side of the stream, then the chameleon moves slowly along it, and to the ground. Nehanda watches it disappear slowly into the grass.

Nehanda hides away in the hills, which are alien to her pursuers. Sometimes the searchers pass her as she sleeps at the entrance to a hidden cave. How could a woman survive this forest? They believe they have searched it thoroughly, but they are deceived. She sees them as they go down the hill, turning into dust.

The searchers, led by Mr Browning, return and harass the villagers, but they still cannot find her. The people insist she is in the hills. With guns pointed at their backs, men from the villages guide the white men through the forest, and into the hills where they have missed her. Mr Browning bounds over the boulders, shooting at antelope when he can, and enjoying a temporary triumph.

Nehanda rises with the sun, which sends blinding yellow rays into her eyes. The dew moves like rain over her feet. She desperately wants to survive another day of telling, and mutters prayers to her departed dead. Her tongue will not rest and fills the forest with echoes of her being. After she has drunk water from a stream she sings. She fights the silence that the strangers have willed upon her. The birds depart into the sky as she moves through the tall *musasa* trees where spider webs reflect the dawn.

There are no longer any sacred spaces on the ground, only shifting spaces temporarily marked by empty gestures in the air: the pursuer swinging his gun from shoulder to shoulder, the victim darting back and forth behind the thick protecting trunks of trees and the salient rocks. Nehanda carries her wisdom with caution, cradling it beneath her breast. She has

crossed the boundary of sleep many times, and of death. Close to the dead, and close to their powerful secrets, she feels no fear of dreams. The spirit from which she is descended has passed on to her a seed which she has planted in the fertile ground. She has clutched it between her fingers for so long. She has been crossing boundaries into a sorrow born out of sacrifice. When she turns her eyes to the sun, red and white light spreads across the horizon.

She walks in circular paths through the forest, in a ritual of another birth. She goes into the cave and banishes her own shadow. In the cave is her second birth. There are no witnesses to her second birth, only the spirits that send elegies to those who have been sacrificed in the fight. She weeps until the stars break into the sky and bring the light back into her eyes, then she watches them dance across the sky, darting, skirting, and exploding, giving birth to other stars, dying in perfect patterns in harmony with their moment of death, knowing that the darkness will vanish as another brightness comes into the sky and destroys them, but speeding themselves to that death, singing in their brief glory which is their triumphant moment, existing in harmony with the darkness that makes them burn.

In the darkness with the flickering fire that keeps her warm through the night, she closes her eyes and calls back her long death-defying journeys through the forest. In each circle that she has woven, she sees the completion of something definite and unconquerable. Each circle is a word which will redeem the soil from the feet of strangers, a trap for those who dare follow her footsteps on the ground along the path to ancient wisdom.

She allows the darkness to protect her like a shield.

21

The huts are arranged in a crescent facing the east. The thatching sags along the edges of the walls. It has aged from a glistening tawniness to a decaying brown. Around the cracked mud walls of the smaller huts the thatching droops to the ground. Chickens peck at it, tossing the stems across the yard to their young. The more aggressive chickens fly in one whirring leap onto the thatching where they will make their nests. The dogs lie beneath the overhanging grass with drooping eyelids, shaking off the flies which settle along their sore-filled ears.

The cooking hut, rounded and low, squats behind the row of huts. It does not carry its seclusion with grace. The once supporting bark which formed knots around each bound portion of thatching grass has snapped and released the grasses. The peak into which the thatching once rose has disintegrated into a flat porous basin, through which thin rays of light reach the hearth at the centre of the hut. The covering mud has fallen off the oblong entrance and the poles shaping the door stand like exposed bones. The ants attack the poles at the back where the sun does not disturb them, eating away the core, then leaving the exterior strikingly patterned with tiny holes. It would take only a single afternoon of light showers to bring down this crumbling edifice.

There is still some life around the settlement, even though most of the men have been gone for months. It is not known if any of them will come down from the hills, or if they do, how much of themselves they will have left behind. In this listless half-life the women continue to work, their pestles pounding half-forgotten rhythms into the earth. They pound the last remaining grains of mealies, picking up the few that fall to the ground before the chickens, equally desperate, get to them. The children play beneath the *hozi* which is now empty of provisions. When they climb over the walls of the

78

empty *hozi* and play inside, no one reminds them of the taboos that accompany such a transgression. Since the fighting has begun, each day stands alone, uninterrupted.

The boy is in the *musasa* tree, in his usual place. Now that there are no more cows, he comes here every morning. First he climbs all the way up to the branch near the top, the highest one that will bear his weight. He leans out until his head emerges from the foliage, causing the top of the tree to bend towards the sun, but he is not afraid. He can see everything that goes on in the village, and he can also survey the hills that descend like steps to the river far below. His sisters are now returning with vessels filled with water on their heads, but they are still two hills away and little more than dots. Since the rains ceased, the springs have dried up and life has become more difficult in many ways.

By descending to the next branch, he can lean the other way and get a view of the higher hills, away from the morning sun. His father is somewhere in those hills. But he can see those hills just as well from the ground, so he descends a stage further, where he can rest comfortably on a thick branch.

From this point the view is restricted, being focused rather narrowly in three directions, determined by the openings in the foliage. He can still see the path to the east leading down to the river. On the opposite side of the tree, he can look down obliquely to see his own hut. And by looking almost straight down, he has a view of a patch of ground just under the tree itself, now occupied by a hen and one chick.

Sometimes he stays on this perch almost all morning. Ants travel up and down the trunk. They seem to be in a hurry. He thinks that the ones going down should jump. He flicks one off. He is unable to follow its flight, but a moment later he sees the hen and the chick make a dash for something.

His sisters have stopped to rest just above the last crest. Each of them now has two legs and two arms. They will be here soon. Above their shoulders two dots approach the river in a cloud of dust. They cross and disappear. His sisters are collecting soil from an anthill. As they assist each other in lifting their vessels back onto their heads, the dots reappear, then melt, then rise. Their size and shape change constantly in the rippling heat.

The boy looks down. The chickens have been replaced by a very thin dog with a sore ear. There are three flies on the sore, and others buzz around it. On the other side of the tree, two women sit outside the hut trying to attach the blade of a hoe to its handle. He can see his aunt but only the hands of his mother. He can tell that the women are performing this task for the first time.

The dots now appear to be two people sitting on cows. The boy observes them with increasing interest. He has never seen people sitting on cows. They have stopped at the place where they may choose to come up to this village or to go to one of the villages farther along the valley. Most of those villages are now empty, however. The people on the cows continue to approach, then disappear, approach, then disappear.

As they come over the last ridge, the boy sees that the animals are not cows after all. The tails swish and he is reminded of the chief's ceremonial fly whisk. His sisters stoop to enter the hut, then emerge a moment later without their vessels and move out of sight. From the ground, the riders are not yet visible.

The boy watches them with growing absorption. He sees that the animals' hair is short and glistening, except along the back of the neck, where it is longer and darker, like the tail. The behaviour of the tail is mesmerizing. Held in a graceful curve, it shakes delightfully at each step, occasionally flicking to one side with a wonderful, smooth elegance. At the point when the animals leave the boy's path of vision, they are entering the village.

The panic on the ground surprises the boy. He now realizes that he should have warned his mother and his aunt, but it is too late. His mother is frantically calling him and his sisters. He starts to move down but then the animals reappear directly below him, where they are tied to the lowest branch. He can see the head of one animal, whose hair is brown, and the tail of the other, which has black hair and is facing in the opposite direction. He is paralyzed by a mingling of fear and fascination.

The commotion increases. His aunt runs into the hut with his sisters, then emerges to stand beside his mother, who blocks the doorway, still holding the hoe. Both women are shouting angrily. The animal whose head he cannot see makes a soft chuffing noise, and the other makes a musical sound, jerking its head up so that he can see one large white eye like a peeled egg.

A very loud, sharp sound rings out. His mother slumps in the doorway and lies still, while his aunt screams and picks up the hoe. The sound is repeated and she too lies still. The branch the boy is holding begins to shake. He grips the trunk instead. Gasping sounds emerge from his throat. The black horse stamps its foot three times.

There is more screaming from further down the village, and the sound of pots breaking, and then the terrible sharp sounds. Later, smoke rises into the tree, and the boy sees flames leaping through the roof of the hut. His body shakes and he is crying and he bites hard to try and stop. After a time he is still shaking but the crying has ceased, and he thinks perhaps the crying was not his.

He can no longer see the river, but he can still see the animals beneath the tree. A fly lands near the shoulder of the brown animal. The skin of the animal shivers, and the fly circles away. He does not want to look at the animals any more, and he closes his eyes. When he opens them, the animals are not there.

In the morning, the river is still there, and the walls of the hut, and his mother and his aunt. He is very cold, and his hands are bleeding, but his arms and legs have stopped bleeding, though he had not known about the bleeding until now. In some places there is pain, but in most places there is not any pain or anything at all. It takes him a long time to climb down without the use of his fingers, and at the end he can only reach the ground by falling.

The smoke is inside him trying to escape, and it is also outside him trying to enter, and he has to concentrate very hard to prevent anything from either entering or leaving. His stomach is as hard and bitter as a *matamba* shell. He feels content that he is without hands, because it limits the opportunities for misfortune. Later, however, he feels that something is leaving him through the end of his arm, and he wakes to find that he does have hands, and that a dog is licking his hand. Still, so many other parts of him are missing that he does not bother to try to get up. The ground under him is covered with the marks made by the feet of the animals which had stood facing in opposite directions. He wishes to die, but he will not die that day.

Later the pain begins, passing in waves from his stomach to his head, and the thirst is terrible. He crawls away from the hut. Sometimes he tries to stand up, and finally he succeeds and after that he is able to move faster. By nightfall he has reached a place where there is no smoke, and as he sleeps each scream is a small victory over terror, and the next day he is stronger.

He moves toward the hills, and later that morning he finds water. The first time he drinks it is not good, but the second time it is all right. He does not die that day either, or the next.

He does not want to see the animals any more, but when he closes his eyes the animals are still there. But he no longer wants to die, and he does not die that year, or the next.

22

The chameleon pauses in the midst of its dance, frightened by the wind. Fearing the arrival of its enemies, it dares not move from the elbow of the tree. It sends a trail of saliva ahead to prepare its precarious passage to the bush beyond.

The air is still and rests on the dry riverbed where all life has vanished. A few pools of muddy water dot the sand where tadpoles struggle to mature and escape. Some say the sun descended stealthily one night and swallowed the earth. The water and the green of the valley were swallowed by the sun, which now watches from a safe distance in the sky. The villagers see dead birds fall from the sky. The wind comes and spreads black feathers across the earth. The people turn away from the smell of the rotting birds.

When Kaguvi surrenders to the settlers and is imprisoned, the villagers are alarmed. The most respected among them sit defiantly outside the walls of the prison. The hunt for Nehanda continues.

Kaguvi does not rest. He moves around the small room, enacting dreams. He is resilient in his fight.

The people return to their villages, most of which have been burnt down. After they have rebuilt their huts, the settlers come and kill half the families, to force the leaders of the rebellion to come down from the hills. Inside the prison walls Kaguvi hears the beseeching voices of the elders, while Mr Browning angrily fires gunshots into the air. The villagers place *mhunga* in clay pots filled with water and make beer for

their ancestors.

"Show us the way."

"Do not abandon us on this difficult path."

"We are your children."

They pray to *Mwari* their god, and send messages to the ancestors by pouring beer into the ground. *Mwari* is the supreme rain-giver, the great mystery of water from which the people seek their faces. The *mudzimu* plead with the ancestors, who approach *Mwari* on their behalf.

The horizon looks back at them with an angry aspect. The redness of the dying sun spreads across the sky. Their prayers will not reach the departed.

"You who are in the ground, do not forget us. Chameleon dances led us across diverse paths, and lent us tongues that reached into the past of our memory. We cannot remember the tongues that have led us to watering spaces, from dew to dew. The earth has abandoned the gifted among us: it has betrayed us with an empty sky."

And the dead are among them, but there is no one to interpret the messages which come from beyond. The wet ground that they have covered with ancestral beer is filled with the disturbing sounds of strange insects. They close their ears to keep out the sound which has been sent from the unknown to confuse them. The women pour more beer on to the ground to appease the ancestors who turn away from them in anger.

"We are not to blame," they cry into their cupped hands. "Our children have died in this fight." They plead without hope of relief.

"Who is the interpreter among us? Let him come forward!" No one dares read the message on the wet ground. Those who have performed the task before withdraw to the back of the circle. The arrow has been sent from some unknown land to destroy them. They do not know how to evade its fatal poison.

"Help us find a way," they plead.

They sharpen their arrows and prepare poisons from wild

fruit.

"Help us against those who have bewitched the sky," they cry.

They look to the heavens in anticipation of their relief, but there is only the barrenness. They raise their arms to the sky and feel the wind move mockingly between their fingers. The wind carries dead leaves across the ground. They dance supplications to the distant moon, from which they witness images of the future. Their feet are covered in dust from their dancing.

The gifted among them play frantically on the drums, until Nehanda is among them with promises of their future. The drum echoes her message and the past is returned to them. Large brightly coloured birds descend from the sky on to their dancing ground.

Soon the birds are covered with dust that rises from the ground.

Soon the birds have melted into the earth.

23

On the path a snake passes. In the morning, its shed skin is bright with dew.

Kaguvi has a habit of sucking in his cheeks, making clicking sounds which inhabit the room like a companion.

On a low wooden table, a book lies open. The paper is thin and transparent, so that the letters of the next page show through. The priest bends over the book. Kaguvi follows the regular movement of the priest's right hand. The fingers move slowly across the open surface of the book from top to bottom, twice, then rapidly to his mouth where they touch the tongue before returning to the corner of the book and turning a leaf. This rhythmic process is accompanied by a nodding motion of the head and upper body. But Kaguvi cannot see what is being put into the priest's mouth, and although he watches for a long time there is no swallowing. Also his eyes are behaving strangely: unlike the rest of his body, their movement is quick and irregular.

The respect with which the priest treats this thing is evident. Perhaps this is his *gano*, the one that a man passes on to his first-born son when he dies. Yet its shape and size do not suggest any immediate usefulness.

Kaguvi inclines his head, to get a better view. "Did you receive this thing from your father?" he asks.

"Yes, this is the work of Our Father."

"What will happen when these leaves turn to dust?" he asks.

The priest answers with a calm patience. "There are many copies of this book, and more can be produced. This book can never die."

Kaguvi scrutinizes both book and man intensely. He is not one to close his mind to a mystery. It is better to know what governs the stranger's world, and what secret fears he holds. Kaguvi does not expect to be charmed by what he will learn.

"My *gano* will help me in battle. How does this thing help you?"

"This book guides and sustains me at all times. It is the mouth of God."

Only his mouth? Kaguvi watches the hand move back and forth. Perhaps it is the opposite of what he had thought. The priest is not the only one who is eating after all. "You have many gods, then . . ."

The priest looks up. He is now animated. "There is only one God," he says.

Kaguvi is fascinated. The priest's god can break into many pieces. But he also feels pity for a god who has to manifest himself in this humble manner. He does not understand why a god would hide behind the marks on a page.

"He is inside your book, but he is also in many books," Kaguvi says. "Your god is strange indeed. My god lives up above. He is a pool of water in the sky. My god is a rain-giver. I approach my god through my ancestors and my *mudzimu*. I brew beer for my god to praise him, and I dance. My *mudzimu* is always with me, and I pay tribute to my protective spirit." Perhaps he can convince the priest that his god is alive too. The priest shakes his head and answers slowly, as though in agreement.

"That is my God too, he is in the sky. But my God is the true God. He is the way to eternal happiness." He points to the roof of the prison, which is very low.

Kaguvi is confused. He has never entertained such an improbable idea as eternal happiness. If a man harvests his crops, that is happiness. If a man marries and has children, that is happiness. If a man talks to his neighbours and they respect him, that too is happiness.

"In heaven we shall find happiness. More happiness than in all the earth. In heaven we shall not labour, we shall sing and rejoice."

"We shall not labour?" Kaguvi asks again, baffled. He does not know why a man would long for that kind of happiness. Work is not suffering, even though the priest insists that work has come into the world as a punishment on one man. What kind if god is this that will not be appeased with beer poured on to the ground? It is not punishment for a man to do all he can for a good harvest. For a man not to labour is laziness.

"Shall we go to heaven to be lazy? To sit behind our huts and bask in the sun like lizards?" he asks suspiciously.

"We shall be kings in heaven. All of us shall have an equal share of happiness." The priest speaks in a sonorous voice and spreads out his arms as though to level out the inequalities in the world. .

"We shall all be kings?" Kaguvi repeats incredulously. This would be a chaotic world indeed. He makes impatient sounds through his cheeks. This was a matter for a man to consider with his kin.

"Your god is an evil god," the priest appeals to him. "I am here to save you from the eternal flames."

The arrogance of the priest is shocking. He has painted pictures of suffering and of hell, but to Kaguvi it all sounds unconvincing. The priest does not bear the aspect of a man who would lie. For Kaguvi, the evidence of a man's worth is also in his face. A man can lie with words, but his body will betray him. It is hard for him to believe that the priest is entirely foolish. There is certainly a tenderness in his smile, and real concern in his voice.

"I know there is life after death," Kaguvi agrees, nodding his head. "But that is life as a spirit, to help protect those who are living." But the priest insists on an afterlife in which men will rise from their graves in their former bodies.

"Bearing even the scars they have received in battle?"

"Yes, in their true bodies."

* * *

The prophetic cloud in the sky has burst for Kaguvi, and there is nothing strong enough left to shelter his dreams. His ancient spirit, which he now sees as something separate from himself, weighs sorrowfully on him. It is as though they now live in separate ages of time, himself in the present, his spirit departing further into the past. They move in both directions of time, and they will not find each other. Before today, Kaguvi has ridden on the back of the spirit. Now he can only see short distances to his right and to his left, backwards and forwards. His dreams are the most terrifying nightmares.

Kaguvi dare not look at the lion which is now crouched at the opposite side of the room, its mane raised angrily until its brown and yellow hairs touch the roof. The lion crouches, ready to attack him. He hears a distant chant call his praise name, "Gumboreshumba . . . Gumboreshumba . . ." But there

88

is no promise there to save him, only a wild echo that has been sent to taunt him. Kaguvi curses and turns his back away from the wall. Kaguvi keeps the voracious eyes of the beast close to his own, and they send mysteries to each other, mysteries that can no longer unite them. All the promises have been broken, and Kaguvi's spirit is naked to his creator, his ruling spirit manifest in the animal. The lion has arrived to prepare him for the next life which he will enter carried in the safety of its belly. He will travel in the belly of the beast for many days, then he will be freed to join his ancestors who have prayed for him from the earth. The lion will outlive him with new lives.

Kaguvi cannot bear to watch himself crouching out there. In the darkness, with the moon sending trembling rays through the square window on one side of the room, he makes out the shape of the sleepless lion which waits for him. Many times he has invoked it, and it has come to his assistance. The lion is his great ancestor bearing in the strength of the right leg all the power of Kaguvi's prophecies. All Kaguvi has been given has been the strength in one of its legs.

The spirit departs in regretful spasms that send Kaguvi crawling from one corner of the room to the next. The blood-feeding spirit roars as it leaves him. Kaguvi's forehead streams with water. His ears sing with deafening, pulsating blood. After the ceaseless pounding in his head, and the burning in his stomach, Kaguvi understands. His name will utterly destroy him. No one can walk away from the departed, free and whole.

When Kaguvi opens his eyes, he sees a dim light on the horizon. The light begins to grow. Kaguvi weeps. The clouds darken.

24

In the caverns the bats hang and give birth in the darkness, struggling to hold on to their newly born who are drawn to the ground. Their perpetual blindness ensures that they are always the newly born. They do not see the corruption of the earth while they float on the dreaming air. Their soothing journeys sway them to an eternal sleep where they meet death – their own death. Always, they are **fin**ding ways of seeing, and of experiencing the air.

The guardian of the caverns had spoken with an alluring voice saying, "Leave your sight in a basket at the entrance of the cavern, and you shall be given shelter." But they have been deceived. Their sight is kept from them. Because they cannot see the horizon the future disappears from their imaginings. Forced to live in the margin of sight they devise elaborate languages to locate their young in the swarming sound-filled roof of the cavern where they wait.

Nehanda hears the sound of the pounding drums reverberate against the walls of the cave, and sees the dancing feet of her people. She calls to her presence the distant drums. Her legs are stretched ahead of her, then folded over each other. Her hands lie separately between her thighs. She is facing the mouth of the cave.

"The blood of your sons and your daughters flows in rivulets across the land. What ritual shall we perform to cleanse the ground before our ceremonies of birth?"

Part of the entrance is blocked by grass. It is dark inside the cave, but she sees the light come in through the narrow opening that forms the entrance. The light falls scattered onto the ground on one side. She can see the sky from one side of the opening, and trees fading into the distance, merging with the horizon. The clouds have dispersed across the sky.

The paleness of the sky combines with the brown grey of the trees so that it all seems one to her. She sees the same sky through the tall sparse grass, which moves regularly with the wind, and the sky itself trembles. She watches the sky from the entrance of the cave, calling to the protectors of the earth. The frenzied drums have become silent, but she continues to hear the voices of ululating women who sing and clap their hands. Their voices echo around her. The women carry babies on their backs. The drums and the people disappear from the clearing, fading suddenly into the ground.

The white rays of light turn to mist, and even the grass she has pushed aside on her way into the cave has disappeared from view. The thick mist fills the walls of the cave, but she fails to see anything in this curiously ambivalent light. The light distorts all shapes. The light of the sky is within her, and she calls to the departed who will protect her from this vision of death. In the mist, which is also the sky, she sees no image of the future.

The mist turns to water and moves down her face and neck, and the darkness is returned to her. In the comforting darkness, the spirits guide her into a sacred place inside the cave. She digs the soft earth with her fingers, and finds a clay pot filled with red soil. The soil has been taken from an anthill.

The pot carries images of the future.

25

She has rubbed animal dung over her legs. On the other side of the river, she sees reflected the living part of herself. In this life it is the dead part of her being which guides her, and which speaks. The river, resting between her being and her non-being, links her to superior forms of existence. She prefers the burden of her seeing self, and will not cross the river to reach its opposite shore. Nehanda sees the sun reflected in the water.

She has travelled long distances through time to meet this vision of the future. She knows that her own death is inevitable, but sees its significance to the future of her people.

In the future, the whirling centre of the wind, which is also herself, has collapsed, but that is only the beginning of another dimension of time. The collapse of the wind, which is also her own death, is also part of the beginning, and from the spiralling centre of the wind's superimposed circles another wind rises, larger and stronger. Hope for the nation is born out of the intensity of newly created memory. The suffusing light dispels all uncertainty, and the young move out of the darkness of their trepidation, into the glory of dawn. The trembling wind asserts its eternal fury, and it will not be dominated, or destroyed. It walks in long furious strides across the clearing, and mocks those in its path with a nodding fantastic head. From its consuming base it digs the earth which it sends speeding into the blinding air. It prepares its own path majestically, as though it has come from witnessing the birth of the earth. Its frantic arms wave in circular protective gestures. Those who see it coming into being understand its message with new light, and they are not afraid. The path has been cleared with wisdom.

In the future, the valley will once again regain its colour and its growth. It will bear new lives, which will be born out of the old. There will be a growth there, among the swinging branches, among the sheltering leaves. Her death, which is

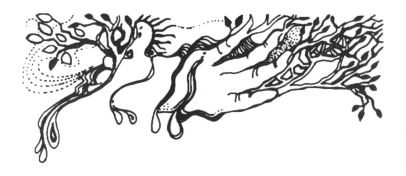

also birth, will weigh on those lives remaining to be lived. In the valley, where they have prayed all night for rain, is heard the beginning of a new language and a new speech. The water rises to their knees, and they dare not move. For many days the water comes to them, and the river is full of sound, and echoes with resonances of eternal mysteries. From the rich green treetops brightly coloured birds fly, and the young boys follow them into openings on tree-trunks where they find honey which they share with the birds. The elders stay along the banks of the river where they have discovered new lives. They have found themselves in the future which they thought they had lost. At the bank of the flowing river where life grows, they bury the dead part of themselves.

The energy that propels the whirling wind rises from a shaft in its belly, which is the hungering centre into which it swallows all obstacles in its path. It sighs with impatient commands, and the birds fly out of the trees bearing signs that send new hope to the ground. It is always in a state of creation, and of being born: the legend-creating wind gives new tongues with which to praise it, and new languages with which to cross the boundaries of time. Out of it evolves new patterns of growth, and new purposes with which to greet the waking day. Each seeks lightness and freedom, guided by the recollection of the death-defying mother of dreams. From dreams come life, and growth. Old men borrow lives from the branches of trees, until they can pass on to the unborn the fantastic images they have witnessed. In cheerful voices the women celebrate their shelter-giving selves, and see new existences come out of the dreaming air. They too are in a state of birth, and growth, and unstoppable exultation. After the agonizing birth they have witnessed they rise from the tattered mat and learn to walk; their footsteps bear signs of a majestic language that will lead them safely into the future. They clap their hands and create new songs to help clear the path into new lives. When they do not sing their lips part, and wait. The air waits to be transformed into the ecstasy of their release. The women see images of themselves reflected in the motionless lake in the sky. With words compelling them through the intersection of time, they recognize their future selves. The women welcome the message of their inheritance and they will not forget: the time of fading truths is gone.

The newly born come into the world bearing gifts. They walk and speak. They have eyes that hold memories of the future, but no one is surprised: they have received their sight back. The newly born come into the world with freed souls that are restless; they seek ways to outwit their rivals. They speak in voices that claim their inheritances. But those to whom they speak have filled their ears with insects. The sky which has betrayed them sends spears of rain into their midst, and they pick them up and cover the plains.

Nehanda sees the future clearly and distinctly, and is fulfilled. But for now, her people will continue to be killed until evidence of her death has been found.

The sun continues to shine across the river.

They find her sitting in a clearing, waiting.

26

Her armpits are filled with cobwebs and she looks up in surprise. An echo reaches her from the sky.

A stream of yellow liquid makes its path toward the entrance of the cell, having made a detour to a stern-looking pair of polished black shoes, a little to the right.

The spider's web blinds her. Outside, the cock crows in circles that unite the earth. Even its echo carries messages from the past, and she is not afraid.

She has turned away from him. Her palms cover her eyes,

trembling, resentful. Mr Browning sits on a wooden bench that has been brought into the room for his convenience. She does not want his presence, and puts her arms across her face. Her eyelids are heavy with sleep.

"So, you refuse to be converted?" he asks.

A wasp has built its home next to the cobwebs, carrying a sting on its back. The wasp moves in and out of her ears, singing of future triumphs. Nothing. I shall tell them nothing. She would not accommodate another people's god. She bites on her tongue and fills her mouth with blood. She rests her bare back against the rough brown mud-covered walls of the prison, which feel cold and dead.

A deep black shadow grows on the wall. It is herself.

A darkness will heal her. Soon. Water gathers around her. Here she is in this prison turning into water. Sinking, almost blind.

Darkness. And let it arrive.

A spider swings back and forth across the light which comes in through the window. Mr Browning moves his feet, curses, leans against the wall. She laughs at his god. Her laughter fills her with secrets of her existence. The sun sends webs into her eyes. She sighs and raises her knees close to her chin.

Mr Browning continues talking.

Her body rocks back and forth, as though she would sleep. She wants to get up and dance, but her shoulders are filled with sleep. She has heard the drums, and now she will dance the histories of her people. She dances against Mr Browning and his God, against these strangers who have taken the land, she dances the faces of her people, the betrayal of time, the growth of wisdom, the glory of their survival – a shadow, moving on the wall. She dances in harmony with the departed who protect the soil from the feet of strangers. Thorns dig deep beneath her feet and she bursts into song.

Then she lets out a scream that sends Mr Browning across

to the other side of the room. Mr Browning is convinced of her madness. He stands away from her, but there is no distance between them. If Mr Browning were to stretch out his hand, he could touch her. But he has come to look, to mock, not to touch. This frail woman has eluded him for so long. Possession. Spirits. Ancestors. He would show her who was possessed.

She follows a meandering path that circles the earth, beyond the lake in the sky, into distances of her future. Nehanda waits while water falls from the sky, falls into song, falls into morning. She sees smoke, risen and old. The water spreads across the earth, in a promise of her relief.

With frantic arms she gestures into the air. She is alone, and the sound of her hands is hollow. There is not a clay pot to be found. Her arms move about the earth, in search of the elusive gourd that holds memories of her being. Some part of herself is buried in the earth, but she can no longer find it. She is alone, and lies still on the ground. In the silence she hears the wind move. The wind carries clouds of decaying leaves and the harsh smell of fresh cow-dung. The wind moves in circles across the ground.

"Kaguvi has been hanged." Mr Browning says.

Her face is cracked, like mud on a dry riverbed.

27

A large cloud of fire leaps into the midst of death. The sky is filled with hissing flames. The fire carries a canopy of dark impenetrable smoke. Yellow and blue flames shoot angrily into the blue sky, tarnishing the heavens. Billowing smoke comes toward the people, carried by the wind. The burning consuming shapes send harsh smoke through the air, which carries the smell of dry grass. The radiance grows larger and larger into ever widening circles, glowing, rippling into the horizon. The flames of the fire disappear in a cloud of smoke, then return with a renewed fury. Shadows vanish from the earth.

"My people will not rest in bondage. The day has ceased too quickly." Her telling awakens the dead part of the living, who are also divine because they are descendant from the departed dead. The living are listeners, the dead are powerful articulators. Only the dead make the living speak. She sees a calabash bearing a circle of black beads. It is covered with a layer of dead grey ash. The calabash is empty and sits abandoned in the centre of a clearing in the forest where a ritual has been interrupted. Black crows stare curiously from the branches of trees.

The daylight finally comes through the opening along the wall, pouring in reluctantly as though in possession of all her secrets. The sun sends a faint shadow which she watches as it climbs the wall. She sees it from a distance beneath the earth. The shadow grows and moves across the beam of light. The shadow will soon be swallowed by the earth.

She welcomes her departed, and the world of her ancestors. The whiteness around her eyes has turned to a redness that is also death. The chasm between the living and the dead is broken. A wave of nausea moves in circles within her, searching.

The wind covers the earth with joyful celebration